T0053834

DOMINIQUE FABRE

My Life As Edgar

translated from the French by
Anna Lehmann

archipelago books

Copyright © Librairie Arthème Fayard, 2005
English language translation © Anna Lehmann, 2023

First Archipelago Books Edition, 2023

All rights reserved. No part of this book may be reproduced or transmitted in
any form without the prior written permission of the publisher.

Library of Congress Cataloging-in-Publication Data available upon request.

Archipelago Books
232 3rd Street #A111
Brooklyn, NY 11215
www.archipelagobooks.org

Distributed by Penguin Random House
www.penguinrandomhouse.com

Cover art : Mauricio Lasansky
Book design: Gopa & Ted2, Inc.

This work is made possible by the New York State Council on the Arts
with the support of the Office of the Governor
and the New York State Legislature.

This publication was made possible with support from
Lannan Foundation, the Carl Lesnor Family Foundation,
and the National Endowment for the Arts.

Printed in Canada

My Life as Edgar

RUE D'AVRON

I WAS A QUIET, unassuming child, but I had features of a kid with Down syndrome – a kind of coldness around the eyes, pale lips, big cheeks, a big butt, though my chromosomes weren't really to blame. I could hear people around me say *He's not all there, is he?* in soft voices, secretively, only I had ears, phenomenal ears, Mickey Mouse was deaf compared to me, nature didn't do me any favors, except for my ears. Nature, it's true, isn't here to do us any favors. I still don't know if I'm all there, but one thing is for sure: from the age of three Maman began to have doubts, and apparently – I don't remember this, it must be another one of the things people let drop within range of my ears – she took me one morning for a consultation at the hospital at Rue d'Avron, where a psychiatrist examined me, a lady I remember very well. She had a white cone in her straw-colored hair and thin-rimmed glasses, the kind that are only half covered by social security, and if my ears were vast receiving stations, with her it was her eyes – blue, a little watery, like the nuns at the hospital at Rue d'Avron – taking in everything at once.

Given that I was only three, her conclusions were not definitive. She asked me lots of questions. No answer. Then she gave me some drawings to do. As far as drawing goes, I was particularly useless, and under her all-seeing gaze, my all-hearing ears began to hear only the squeaky sounds I was making with the tips of the Caran d'Ache colored pencils she'd borrowed from the hospital at Rue d'Avron.

"Sweetie, are you done?"

Maman followed my efforts at making a nice drawing with her dark and ever-traumatized gaze, I must have been torn – no, I was *torn* – split in two between the desire to make nice pictures and the desire to keep making the Caran d'Ache pencils squeak, to fill my head with sounds, not because I like music, not even the music of the pencils. I was, I am still, quite stupid about music, despite my quasiseismographic ears, good only for picking up small tremors of course. The waiting room wasn't full, far from it, yet I wasn't the only quiet, unassuming child in the Paris area in 1964, and if on top of everything else I weren't hopelessly lazy, I'd describe to you in one go everything you need to know about 1964, and should the next year rear its head, as soon as I heard the sadistic pop of the champagne corks on December 31st – while hugs and wishes were exchanged – I'd take advantage of the slightest lull to inflict 1965 on you. And so on and so forth. It goes to show I won't have lived in vain. In fact, there were three children in the waiting room at Rue d'Avron, a fat little girl with a double-chin, greasy hair, glasses, and encephalitis and a skinny little boy with arms that hung down like a monkey's, who was all rigged up with bifocal glasses and hearing aids, a genuine Down syndrome case this time. So I didn't do the drawings that would've allowed Mme. Clarisse Georges to determine in what way I wasn't all there, but I gave her a hug at the door because I was very into hugging in those days, I still am, often when I'm not paying attention, my tongue sneaks out of my mouth on its own. Then we left the hospital at Rue d'Avron. I was born at a Catholic institution, and it was no doubt out of Christian charity that Mme. Clarisse Georges didn't tell my mother straight out what she already knew, what all the nuns already knew, that I was off to a rough start in life.

I didn't have the normal curiosity of a child my age, I was already deceitful, a far cry from the kind of sweet little boy who takes you back to your own childhood. But I wasn't a real pest either. I was quiet, unassuming, pudgy, with skinny arms and legs, it was only much later that I wore glasses like the little fatty in the waiting room. I didn't know how to draw, I didn't know how to stack cubes, I didn't even know how to babble or how to stop crying when I cried, I never laughed, in fact, I didn't know how to laugh, I didn't know how to wear Maman's shoes without falling on my face, I didn't know how to stick my tongue back into my mouth, I didn't blush, I didn't turn white as a sheet, either, given my natural complexion. Only my ears worked to full capacity, night and day. We came out of the hospital where I was born, Rue d'Avron, and Maman was in a hurry. I wasn't. There were things to hear, formidable shrieks filtering down from the midwives' floor.

I could hear the widow Marguerite Perron, who brought me into this word by pulling on my ears because I had a big Down head, say to another mother, it's a boy, girl, I wish you luck. Then she said something like, what did I do with the thread, we'll sew you back up ship-shape, and thank God I wasn't all there because otherwise I'd have passed out, but Maman would have caught me, and we would've no doubt gone back up to the doctor's office pronto. There is, after all, a time when you have to leave your birthplace. It's much better that way. Ouch, ouch, it's nothing, girl, what are you going to call this little monster? Ouch, ouch, OOOUUUUCH, we can't decide between Edgar and Vincent, Ouch, and is the papa happy? YEEEEEEESSSSSSSS, enjoy, ouch, have mercy sister, enjoy it while it lasts. Youch. But just then my ears got blocked up because Maman and I were already on the bus, whose number escapes me. We sat down, me next to her, it took us a long time to get back home.

So there it is, what I want to talk about is my quiet, unassuming childhood. In 1964, my silence worried Maman a lot, and also my ears. I had terrible chronic double ear infections. At first she thought my ears, which were constantly inflamed, would diminish in surface area once I wasn't sick anymore. She put a blue knit hat on my head to keep it from cold air, from warm air, from dust. And then she didn't know what to think. In the summer too – I remember the summer of 1964 well, one of the hottest since my birth, maybe the hottest ever – although I was a quiet, unassuming child, I was capable of having terrible tantrums if I wasn't taken to the playground at least once a day. That summer, we took the bus and then the métro to Parc Monceau, one of the wealthy neighborhoods close to our own dirty little suburb, Maman had expensive tastes. She wanted us to stroll, the two of us, among the tots with little blond heads and blue eyes and English nannies. My stroller was a Baby-Roller brand. I don't remember at all what it looked like, but I remember the word baby-roller, in sentences like: where did you find this baby-roller, don't stow the baby-roller near the mailboxes, it was navy blue, like my hat, with two positions, reclined and fully reclined. I must have been in the reclined position since I'd already had a nap.

I loved listening to the birds in the trees in Parc Monceau, as well as the squeaks of moles in the abandoned chalk quarries and the conversations in the quiet, softly carpeted offices that ringed the park. Maman paraded her weariness around, pushing my roller, she must have been bathed in sweat, with her watery look of despair, which now that it's all over sometimes makes me want to hurl myself in front of the stroller that'd cost her half her paycheck, to rip off once more the dark blue hat with pompoms that immediately pointed to her as the one responsible for this human failure and leave with her for a place of clear silence. But in 1964, given that I was not all there, only she noticed the stares, evenly divided between suspicion and disgust, that came our way as we walked. As for me, I mostly remember the strange reactions of the English nannies, they always said things like oh maïe Gawwd, oh maïe Loood, Djiiiises! Maman was not good at foreign languages, despite being a shorthand typist. But I – with my ears stuffed with cotton balls and the usual gunk that filled them, held in place by my hat – I was delighted and, in 1964, before I could speak common words like maman, pee-pee, poop, the only things I

9

could repeat with unfeigned pleasure were the words I heard the nannies say, those horrified little cooing cries they let out whenever they happened upon us. More than one turned her little angel toward the duck pond at the sight of us, Maman and me. We'd stroll around the pond once or twice, and then Maman would make her way (I could feel the courage it took her) toward the playground. In the stroller net where she'd put our things, she hadn't forgotten the bucket and shovel, the baby-bottle of grenadine and, for her, a novel. Maman feverishly devoured the same unbelievable stories where a well-to-do man meets a beautiful working-class woman with lots of good qualities in a public square – not that such things didn't happen, I heard of them too, but if I'm not careful, you won't know what happened in the sandbox at the playground, near Avenue des Ternes, if I start repeating what I heard of the meeting between the rich man and my penniless maman. Because even in 1964 shorthand typing at night school was not a big money-making skill, it was less profitable than accounting for example, or even better, a quick blow job in the alley by the swings, because we met our share of lechers, Maman and I, in 1964. Don't believe that indecent proposals are anything new, patience, patience.

Even if I lack an ordinary memory, I must say that Maman was very beautiful, not that her ears were small but the rest of her was admirably proportioned. So it was that most men sitting on the green benches of Parc Monceau, waiting for a nanny or an opportunity, were quite willing to move aside to give her a spot. That day, we settled out of the sun for my snack, two *Petits-suisses*, a strong dose of antibiotics for my serious ear-infection, the baby-bottle of grenadine. Then she handed me the bucket and shovel and helped me down into the sandbox, where I remained seated, every day of the last two weeks of August 1964, for hours and hours, listening to what was going on. I sometimes ran into the same children: if I closed my eyes I would recognize them. They didn't interest me as much as the English nannies, how I loved the English nannies, their little whispered exchanges about life, the respective merits of Kent or Neuilly, the wealthy neighborhoods, the deviant sexuality of the French. I was really quite happy in the sand. Sometimes, if I felt someone staring at me, I'd try to put sand in the bucket with my shovel, generally without success. Or, I would look at Maman, sometimes waiting with tears in my eyes for a little sign from her, that's good, yes, the shovel, use your hand not your nose. Sometimes I just looked at her. She sat there with her legs crossed, her little black handbag with the gold clasp next to her, the strap still on her shoulder and her book open to page 110, for example (I was never sure), a book she'd covered in white paper because she hated when people read labels, even the titles of novels. She was secretive, but with ears like mine, you can imagine.

Nothing truly noteworthy happened in the sand at Parc Monceau that summer of 1964, except at the end. We went there for nearly two weeks, and eventually, despite my not being all there, I more or less managed to fill the bucket correctly, I enjoyed it there actually, I liked hearing the sand flow like a million little flayed bugs, they suffer until the end, and then it starts over. Maman noticed my progress, which had already given me an erection, when toward the end of our holiday at Parc Monceau she raised her eyes toward me and smiled.

Sometimes it was because of Françoise Sagan, whom she devoured, and at other times, maybe, because of my new-found dexterity with the shovel and bucket. I never played with the other children. But, on that day, I don't know what came over her, Maman stepped into the sandbox in her high heels and squatted down, sitting on her heels, and began to play with me, which set off a roaring in my ears that drowned out the whirr of words all around. Oh! That little monster is hers, poor woman, maïe Gaawwd, Djiiiises, it takes courage. I trembled with indignation, you'd have thought she was deaf. She picked up the shovel, filled my bucket, and once it was filled to the top I slowly poured the sand over my sandaled feet. We did the same thing several times and, when she saw that I was sweating, she removed my hat. I didn't hear the remark that made her jump to her feet and charge, throwing my shovel at the head of little Jonathan, who was cared for by Miss Smith, and demand an apology for what she'd just heard from that unwed mother in her miniskirt, her black hat with its felt ribbon around the crown, her hands covered in a bunch of rings with blue and green diamonds. And, it was then, in 1964, that I regretted that I wasn't all there for the first time in my life. Instead of applauding her – even with my notorious lack of coordination I might have managed, worst of three, to join both hands – I started to cry, which practically never happened, given how quiet and unassuming I was.

Then things got out of hand. The unwed mother from the neighborhood called out to her friends for help; I started to stuff my mouth with sand by the fistful. Maman bashed her on the head with her book, and she came back swinging her Pierre Cardin handbag, but a man soon intervened.

"Ladies," he said, "please, you are making a spectacle of yourselves, this is 1964."

I gulped and looked at him. He was at least twice as tall as Maman.

"Bitch, whore, working-class tramp!"

The unwed mother sashayed back to Jonathan, wiggling her rear end because of the high heels. I stopped crying. The man wasn't in uniform. I might not have been all there, but I recognized police officers, garbagemen, firemen, the park's groundskeepers – this guy was from another planet. He wore a white shirt, unbuttoned at the collar, a silk tie from the men's department of Bon Marché stuck out of his pocket. I can't remember the brand of his jacket. His watch was huge. So were his feet.

Now that the minx in the sandbox had cleared off with Jonathan, Maman was breathing heavily, her cheeks and ears red, her head high, her traumatized gaze directed at the stranger.

"My name is Bernard."

She swallowed painfully, glancing in my direction.

"Thank you, Monsieur."

"Here, if you want to dry off."

I heard her say no, but she didn't dare. I heard her throw herself into my arms, but she didn't dare do that either. I heard her pull my hat onto my head with the kind of energetic and desperate gesture that I had come to love out of habit. I was used to it.

*

Soon Maman took Bernard's handkerchief. It was light blue. She mopped her brow with a light, hesitant gesture, and then I heard her wonder, but what should I do with the handker-

15

chief now, should I give it back to him or not, what do I do, my God help me, the kid's bawling. . . Should I wash it and return it in the mail? But where does he live?

"Keep it," said Bernard.

He turned toward me. Now I could hear him working it out in his head: she's discombobulated over the handkerchief, what's the deal with her kid, ah yes, look at the jug handles on him. She shouldn't cut his hair so short if she doesn't want people mistaking him for a mutant cocker spaniel. He has a weird look. Might even be a mongoloid, it looks like. Too bad. I want her. He bent down toward me.

"What's your name?"

I gave him all the silence I could muster.

"What's his name?"

He turned toward Maman, who was still gripping his handkerchief, though her breathing had calmed.

"Edgar."

"Edgar. Hello Edgar."

The giant smiled at me. He could care less about my not being all there, my name, or my ear infection, aggravated by the sand that Jonathan. . . Oh, right, it was all coming back to me, this had all started between Maman and the other lady when I'd gotten into a fight with Jonathan. He'd tried to take away my pail. He'd made fun of my hat when I put it on, and my ears when Maman took it off.

"Are you ok?"

"Moo. . . Edgar, Edgarrr," I bellowed to scare him.

Then I raised my head, where was she?

I got up and ran toward her.

Something was about to happen but there was nothing I could do, I wasn't all there. I pulled the handkerchief from her hands and tried to tear it up.

"Edgar," whispered Maman. "No."

"Let him be," said Bernard. "Let him get it all out. Tell me Edgar, what is your mother's name?"

I gave him my stupid look. This time Maman did not hesitate.

"My name's Isabelle."

I heard something extremely unpleasant at that moment. Maman's name was Isabelle. Isabelle. I was so quiet and unassuming that I finally gave the man back his handkerchief. Isabelle, Isabelle? My ears kept singing Isabelle to me. I didn't make a fuss when he took my hand, at the end of Edgar and Isabelle's holiday, before, a little before, just a little before, my papa was called Bernard.

So it was that in August of that year, I went with Maman and Bernard for the first time ever to a café and sat at a table outside. I'd already heard Maman thinking about it sometimes, but something always held her back. She was very shy and going to a café cost money. And then, even at an outside table, she was afraid I'd start bellowing – at times sounds would plunge me deep into despair, sounds whose strangeness deafened or terrified me. And then again, from time to time, some other kid or a mother or a man passing by would give an appalled glance at my hat. Maman herself had suffered a lot in her youth because of her ears, even though they were half the size of mine. I might not have been all there, but enough of me was to understand that. As she was putting me to sleep, she would turn her somber, pensive gaze to my face and oftentimes her eyes, our eyes, would simultaneously mist over. The whites of her eyes would redden and seem to drown, her mascara acting as a dam, while my own tears flowed without stop down to my mouth, which was always slightly open because of my lolling tongue. She then had to do something, Maman couldn't stand for me to gulp down my tears while looking at hers. Usually, she went looking for her handbag from 1964 – it dated back to my birth, I know that because I'd heard the midwife Marguerite Perron yell at her in the delivery room, no one is going to steal from you here, girl, as a matter of fact you would have been better off giving birth anonymously in the foster system, think about it next time, push girl, put some effort into it, oh wow, he's got such a big head, the forceps will never fit, the handbag, put it down will you – and then she'd come back with a hand-kerchief, one of those good old lace handkerchiefs she used so often because every time I got an ear infection I'd also come down with a cold, of course, and she had allergies. When we left with Bernard, who was holding my hand, I was immediately on the alert because I was crying my eyes out, swallowing more than my share of sand and mosquitoes from the Parc Monceau. We were going in the direction of Rue du Rocher, Maman didn't seem to notice. He was walking between us and even though I licked and bit the synthetic fabric of his pants once or twice, Bernard pretended not to be upset.

"Edgar, are you biting me? Tell me, how many teeth do you have?"

When we stopped on the sidewalk, I watched the two of them, her and him, unable to understand why she didn't grab Mme. Sagan's book, open to page 110, and give him a good whack with it. It was the first time a giant had ever ignored me, instead of leaning over to peer inside my ears with a headlamp like the ones coal miners have, or asking me to draw something. We were in the street. My heart started to beat very fast because there was a fire station farther down, and firemen were among the people I liked. Bernard packed me into the stroller to cross the street without asking Isabelle's permission. That's when he proposed going to the café, since it was still very hot.

"May I buy you a drink?

Maman blushed. She was very fair, and when she blushed it often began at the back of her neck. My heart was beating.

"The little one, he isn't used to it. I don't know if. . ."

Bernard turned to me.

"How 'bout a Coke, Edgar?"

I bawled a little, not too loud, because I was trying, same as every day for the two weeks we'd been going to the park in the afternoon, to keep my ears peeled for a fire somewhere.

"I don't know if. . . said Maman. Maybe some other time."

"But when?"

"Poop, poop, I have to poop!" I insisted in turn.

Isabelle leaned down toward the stroller, her gaze as dark and traumatized as ever. I could feel my face swelling up fast, somewhere I heard a siren.

"Quick!"

Maman stood up, and now Bernard leaned over.

"I. . . Edgar is acting strange." *My God, have mercy, the kid's going to have a tantrum, I have to get him to Rue d'Avron. Lord, have mercy*, she thought.

Bernard patted me through the soaking wet hat. He removed it gently. Sometimes I still hear the wool scratching over my ears.

"Don't worry, Isabelle. Edgar doesn't look that sick. It's probably just hay fever. Come on, Edgar, hold it in just a little longer, I'm taking you to the café."

That is how, on August 28, 1964, I discovered, one after the next, first the men's room and then Coca-Cola – and, as though that weren't enough, now I was seized with boundless admiration for Bernard, who, even though he wasn't wearing a uniform, intervened at the top of Rue du Rocher to save an old lady. This lady had fainted right in front of the terrace of the café, as though it had been planned. Maman followed us to the glass door of the bar, with her energetic and desperate stride, the same one she had in the mornings when she took me to my caregiver, Auntie Cartier, before rushing off with the same stride, three doors down, from Porte d'Asnières to Porte de Neuilly, because she worked there in a glass building where, from the outside, all one saw were shadows. Bernard had lifted me out of the stroller and was carrying me in his arms. I was working on being all there as hard as I could because the fire truck was getting closer.

"Here, Isabelle, take this table, there's a parasol. Wait for us, we'll be back."

Maman's gaze clouded before my eyes. The fire truck stopped right in front of the café. I was sitting on an off-white toilet, I didn't have to go.

Bernard had closed the door because I didn't want him to watch, but I could hear him speaking, even though his mouth was closed. *She's afraid of everything, he was saying to himself, her kid's sick. She's beautiful, she doesn't know she's beautiful. But she's so beautiful.*

"Hey Edgar, what's up? Are you coming out?"

I trembled with excitement for the first time in my life. I'd never been so close to the firemen from Rue du Rocher. Sometimes, some of them whistled when Maman walked by with the baby-roller. I loved their ladders, I loved to watch them power-wash their red trucks. I loved to hear Isabelle flinch, her emotions clenching shut each time they catcalled her. I, of course, couldn't whistle; I wasn't normal enough for that. In fact, even today, I still don't know how. I stuttered to the giant.

"There are firemen upstairs, quick, carry me."

"What are you talking about?"

"Firemen, quick, back upstairs!"

The heat was infernal on August 28, 1964. When I got back upstairs, Maman was crouched in front of an old lady, the back of her neck white. From where I was in the arms of the giant, I couldn't see the face of the sick woman – maybe she was dead. Bernard sat me down on a white iron chair under the parasol. My ears itched. Three firemen brought out all kinds of shiny metal suitcases. Maman heard us coming; a flyaway strand of hair lay across her face just under her dark and traumatized gaze when she turned toward me.

"Quick, Bernard, something must be done."

I couldn't speak.

"What's happening?" Bernard asked the firemen.

"The lady's heart stopped."

"I can help you. I'm a surgeon, but I still remember how to do a good old cardiac massage from my years as an intern. Isabelle, take my jacket. Go to Edgar, tell him not to panic – I'm right here."

"Yes, doctor," answered Maman. She picked up his jacket and looked around for me.

24

The old lady was really in a bad way. I squinted, torn between my admiration for Dr. Bernard and the sad revelation that my mother's name was Isabelle. Nothing would ever be the same. I knew that Isabelle was a little embarrassed around the edges having a kid like me. She returned to the table holding the jacket. She was terrified for the old lady, whose hairdo was a little pink, no doubt like all the funny old ladies who managed to faint at the top of Rue du Rocher on August 28 at 5 pm. Maman sat back down next to me, her pace brisk, on the verge of panic. I wanted to grab her hand for a transfusion of thereness. I shared her suffering, my ears turned up to the max, so I could keep her up to date on the old lady's palpitations. Next to us, the barman wouldn't take our orders. He was very old too. In those days, barmen in uniform made me think of a type of firemen, demoted for not having been able to save a dying old lady. He wore a bowtie and a vest with dandruff on it, his hair was totally gray.

"Maman, is the lady going to die?"

"No, sweetie, be quiet, please."

I heard Isabelle praying. We were fervent Catholics, Maman and I, because we were poor and praying didn't cost anything. Bernard was kneeling hard on the dead woman's chest. A fireman placed a large tube in her mouth. Maman had tears in her eyes, but not like when we looked at each other in the evening. *If he saves her, I'll sleep with him, I'll sleep with him, I'll sleep with him.* I also heard the old lady dreaming about the ducks in Parc Monceau; she was wondering what year it was. Of course, I knew. All of a sudden, she rose up, sitting on the sidewalk, completely stiff, her pink hair barely mussed. Bernard smiled in Isabelle's direction.

"What year is it, sir?"

Then she immediately lay down again.

The firemen were nice to her. For example, when she wanted to get up to go see the ducks before closing time at Parc Monceau, they brought a kind of bed without wheels on which they carried her to their truck. At that, Maman smiled through her tears. She looked at me, her dark gaze, traumatized since the day of my birth, stopped being traumatized, and she gave my left ear a quick little pull because she was happy.

"He saved her, can you imagine, Edgar?"

I smiled like never before. It was the best day of the best holiday of my life.

"Wait for me, sweetie."

I didn't answer because the firemen had turned on the siren again. I'll be a fireman for old ladies when I grow up. Maman will never die. In the meantime, I watched her return the jacket to Bernard. She discreetly glanced at the tag: the jacket was worth a third of her gross annual pay, the cut was English. John Lennon had worn one like it the year before.

"Here."

"Ah, yes, thank you, Isabelle."

They looked at each other. I felt a little like biting and crying because I could hear everything they were saying to each other. First my mother: *I can't believe a guy like this exists, I've never met a man like this, why would he want me, other than to sleep with, I can't believe what's happening to me, and with the kid in tow too. Here he is. Lord my God, have mercy.*

You, he answered. *You have seen life's dark colors, but now I'll show you the colors of the rainbow. I'll give up sleeping with English nannies because from now on I'm going to sleep with you. No more, no less. You know, I really thought the old lady was a goner, but I felt an aura. And your kid, aside from that retarded look of his, isn't really too much of a pain.*

They walked back slowly, while the barman nodded and grabbed the tray he'd set down. Bernard took a chair. Maman huddled under the parasol next to me. I couldn't hear the firemen's siren anymore.

"What would you like Isabelle?"

Maman took a panicked look at the list the waiter handed her. Any mistake could be fatal, Maman probably hadn't been to a café since I was born.

"A Perrier, please."

"Ah yes, a Perrier, good idea. Two," said Bernard.

"What's the old woman's name?"

Bernard smiled at Isabelle, and turned to me.

"I don't know. But, if she's all right, you know, it's a little bit thanks to you, Edgar. I hadn't heard the fire-truck siren. It was just in the nick of time. Would you like a Coke?"

I looked at Maman. She still had the same dark gaze, but otherwise, I didn't recognize her.

28

"It's good you know."

"Well ok."

We stayed there for a long time. I liked Coke, actually. I heard Isabelle talking, she answered yes, she showed interest, yes, yes. Bernard worked a lot. He did complicated procedures. He came to Parc Monceau because he used to go there before with his own mother. I listened to the sounds around me and finished my Coke to make the giant happy. The two were taking their time. I felt like going back to Asnières, where Maman and I lived. After a while, my ears grew tired. I'd have really liked to go to the hospital at Rue d'Avron to make the Caran d'Ache pencils squeak in Mme. Clarisse Georges' office. Bernard. I was going to have problems with Bernard, I could tell. The old lady, it turned out, actually croaked on August 28, 1964. When I'd last seen her, the dust was already settling in her pink hair. It was the first time I'd ever seen a dead woman. She still had one eye open, it was all white. And, in case you hadn't guessed, my papa Bernard was neither a doctor nor a fireman; he worked as an accountant in one of the offices on Rue du Rocher. He hadn't been able to do anything at all. Maman had covered my eyes, but I'd heard everything through her hands. After it was over, Bernard walked us to Gare Saint-Lazare. The following night he was to come for dinner at our house. As for me, at the end of the holiday, I had a double ear infection and still wasn't all there. They shook hands for a long time.

The holidays were over. I had enjoyed Parc Monceau, I'd had Maman all to myself for nearly two weeks, and despite having met my papa Bernard, she only had eyes for me because we lived alone. To get to the park we took the bus and the métro and we returned by train. I particularly enjoyed listening to the sounds at Saint-Lazare. There were hundreds of people, and in the departures area, above the clock, they all talked at the same time. Things were happening that summer of 1964. Sometimes, the news was worrying, especially the heat wave. Maman often bought a magazine at the newsstand nearest Rue de Rome, which was run by a lady who must have been twice her age. In the sitting position in the baby-roller, I populated my ears with those thousands of words and the sounds of the automatic whistles that worked without attendants in uniforms. We always went to the same train car on the way back. The baby-roller often made it hard for her to board the train, and even though I was quiet and unassuming, as I'd always been, I sometimes grew impatient. Maman's ears would turn red, she'd place Françoise Sagan and her magazine about world celebrities in my hands. After that, once she had managed to lift us on board, she'd sit on a jump seat, one of those good old jump seats from 1964 that took on the shape of a traveler's behind, gleaming in the interminable sunset at Pont-Cardinet. The screeching rails when we exited the dark tunnel gave me stomach cramps, on top of making my ears flinch like crazy.

Maman never touched her novels on the train. Instead she thumbed through her magazines distractedly, only lifting her eyes at the station stops. Occasionally, she'd nod her head in someone's direction because she knew one or two people by sight, usually neighbors on their way home to Asnières by way of Saint-Lazare. I'd prepare to explode on the inside when, right after the next stop, the Seine appeared, with its own quiet and unassuming ways, its barges, and all the way at the end, toward the sun, the first skyscrapers began to show up, little skyscrapers at La Défense, that of course made me dream of thousands of jackhammers at the same time. Maman also gazed at the Seine. We lived on the other bank, and the skyscrapers were a signal that the train would stop at our station next. I'd observe her dark and traumatized gaze, lost I don't know where in the depths of the water, and then after a few seconds, she'd give a little sigh. I'd brake as hard as I could on my baby-roller so the conductor would stop, the one with the large tool bag to repair breakdowns at home. Maman released the brake on the stroller when I'd succeeded in stopping the train. Just as we always took the fourth car on platform 6 on departure, we were always the last ones on the platform coming back. Although I was quiet and unassuming and exhausted from the fun I'd had, she still didn't risk climbing down to the underground tunnel until the train coming from the opposite direction had also departed. The old bottle-green paint on the wooden benches smelled like urine because men have a habit of pissing in train stations. My ears could hear all the way to the Seine at least, in 1964.

My geography was taking shape. Wherever we went, Maman and I always made our plans long in advance - to doodle at the hospital at Rue d'Avron, to visit the Parc Monceau, or even, from time to time, to "go to Paris" as she would say. Because Maman had a maman too, an old woman who wasn't dead and wasn't even very old. But we didn't go often to visit Maman's maman, because they didn't get along. We'd take the underground tunnel, and Maman, who always wore high heels like she did for shorthand typing night classes, had a hard time with the baby-roller. She'd reach the bottom totally out of breath, and then we'd buy bread. She always got *bâtards*. I would stay next to my luxury stroller, right at the entrance of the boulangerie, which didn't have much going for it except for the pastries. We were both quiet and unassuming on those late afternoons. The trains made a terrible racket, worse than the Caran d'Ache pencils, worse than the jumble of passersby at Saint-Lazare. After a while, I'd have totally had it. She'd come out with her gaze dark and traumatized, look around for me and, since I was only three, give me only two smacks for not waiting for her in front of the boulangerie. She'd smack me on Avenue de la Marne and again in the square where the tall guy with ears like cabbage leaves, taller than Bernard, bald, and made of bronze, seemed to be counting the paper clips in his pockets or nonchalantly scratching his balls. Every time, I asked her who he was, she'd reply:

"It's the General, sweetie."

He had a funny mug. He was the President of France. Pigeons liked him, though, and so did I, because Maman always told me his name with a smile. Yes, I liked the old guy. Seeing him put her in a good mood, she'd sing softly for a brief moment – for example, on the evening we met Bernard. But a single glance was enough for her dark and traumatized gaze to take over again, as if someone in the glass building had just told her off. Maman often arrived late for work in the morning after dropping me off at Auntie Cartier's. Isabelle was born in 1937, just before the war the General won. We went home, we lived in a solid building from 1964, whereas along the path the train took, the old buildings in Clichy, puny and blackened by the trains, trembled under my ears in a roar so terrible it was not fit for an unwed mother and her kid to hear. Even in Paris, in the Ménilmontant neighborhood, going up to her not-old mother with an equally traumatized but blue-glazed gaze behind the butterfly frames, I held on tight to the rickety handrail and her hand. Maman had long thin very white hands, generally they were as cold as her feet, except when we climbed the rickety stairs in Ménilmontant, which were also slippery, on Sundays at twelve fifteen. Then her hands were sweaty, I didn't know why.

Once home from the park, Maman gave me my bath. The bath was a moment blessed by God, she'd slip a kind of plastic bag over my hair, and I'd stay there for a good while . . . Then it was time to eat, shit, piss, and head off to bed. It was in general after I'd gone to bed that we started to look at each other in earnest, peering deep into each other's eyes, and often hers were filled with tears. As soon as she closed the door, I started to listen as hard as I could, no matter how loud I bellowed, Maman would always close the door. She had several activities while I slept. Sometimes she did the ironing – she was afraid my ears would get caught in the cord if she ironed while I was still in the room, other times she washed our clothes, flipping on the radio to catch all the evening news. And after that, super late, while I slept recharging the batteries for my ears, she received phone calls. Hello, yes? Yes, yes. Maman wasn't the same when she spoke on the phone, we got it the year before, in 1963, a gray one like you sometimes see when people refuse to upgrade because they want the same people to call them as before. She was so secretive, Maman. On the phone, her voice turned cheerful like when she encouraged me at the hospital at Rue d'Avron so that I'd make pretty drawings, or she'd get the giggles and lose control, as though the statue of the General had come to life and called her from the phone booth near the train station. The train station was right in front of the cinema, where I went much later and got the worse shivers in my ears of my life, except when I heard Maman turn the pages of her Françoise Sagan novel, reread a few lines and return the book to its place on the shelf, then tiptoe on naked toes to the front door at the stroke of midnight to let my papa Bernard in.

"Isabelle, darling."

"Good evening, Bernard, finally you are here, ah you are here." Maman's voice was as excited in the dim light as if

I'd finally learned to speak, apart from words signifying my basic needs.

"Is Edgar asleep?"

"Hold on, take off your jacket, make yourself comfortable. I'll go check."

"Yes."

Bernard too had a funny voice, in fact he had several voices. He also had several lives, and when Maman came into my room, I made the great fatal error of 1964: I rolled over in my bed. I instantly went into a maximum alert nightmare, where the old pervert from the train station square pulled the eyes of Mme. Clarisse Georges out of his pocket and began to put them in Maman's head instead of her own. Maman rushed into my room, placing her hand on my forehead – but with the strong dose of antibiotics I'd taken, I hadn't had time to trigger a fever. Isabelle sat on the side of my little bed in her baby-doll nightgown. She smelled so nice, she'd ironed it the night before, after washing my bottle and her plate, then she'd done crosswords to fall asleep, but it hadn't worked.

And then the phone rang, barely even once – she was already on the white wooden chair next to the phone.

"What's the matter, Edgar?"

I bawled softly to scare her. I had one eye closed and one half-open like the pink-haired old lady who'd wondered what day it was. I listened a little more, wondering how long she'd stay with me while Bernard was outside, ducking his head so as not to hit it against the ceiling. He was examining the tip of his shoes. Now I tuned into him listening back at me, listening to Maman and me together.

He's having a dream, she isn't going to fall for it, is she? He must sleep very soundly with that big head of his. All kids dream. Should I go or not? I came over to sleep with her, sleep with her, but she's driving me crazy, and her Edgar is getting on my nerves. If only he could speak.

Please sweetie, you're my sweet love, you know that. We're in 1964, Bernard might be the love of my life. He saved the pink-haired old lady, and he'll save you too.

Then my eyes rolled upwards under my closed eyelids. What did all this have to do with me?

In reality, Bernard had brought me a truck. He was the one who'd tiptoed in to see me while I slept, his feet as big as the legs of an extension ladder. He hadn't been able to have dinner with us, so he'd come later. We'd waited for him, Maman and I, with tears in our eyes.

"Hi Edgar, here, a fire truck." He showed me how it worked. "Sweet dreams, little one."

Maman waited for him, smoking her evening Craven.

"Yyyeeess," I said.

Bernard closed the door.

"No," whispered Isabelle, "leave it ajar, he'll wake up otherwise."

I fell asleep right away, it was already September.

The two of them made a pretty big racket, we even had complaints. The sound woke me up too. But I didn't dare go out because of the dark. In my room in Asnières, I was always in the dark, except for my ears. Since I was seriously bored, I finally climbed the fire truck ladder and threw myself onto my bed. The next day, Sunday, Bernard went out to buy croissants. I'd thought long and hard during the night. Would I have known what to do if I'd been all there? Sometimes I got fed up with hearing. Still and all, we had a nice day. Isabelle was cheerful, and Bernard liked kids. In fact, he had two more stocked away with his wife, in Levallois-Perret, in an apartment near City Hall.

*

It was shortly after that, if I close my eyes tight to remember, that Maman started to lose it. I don't remember well, but I think things were better before Bernard, at least until the end. In September, I returned to Mme. Cartier, every morning it was a rush with Maman over the Seine, with no one paying attention to anyone else. From my caregiver's building, you could see where the Seine had become ugly. There were other children with me at Auntie Cartier's, but they didn't count, I didn't go to school, because of not being all there and my ears. I was like a package in Maman's arms. I had a hard time walking in the morning on the bridge in Asnières, Isabelle's gaze was dark and traumatized because every morning she saw the Seine and the bridge while holding her Edgar package, and again every night after work. Auntie Cartier, as the kids called her, cleaned her house and gave us candy so we wouldn't be a pain in the ass while she washed. She had her old man Pierrot, who was always in the bedroom because he couldn't stand the kids' screaming. He was always scratching his hairy bellybutton. Very often, I also saw Auntie Cartier's legs, which had something like little black snakes on their backs that are called varicose veins. As for Uncle Pierrot, he wore a navy-blue mariner cap, even when he smoked on the bed in the room where we weren't allowed to go, gazing at the ceiling, his eyes moist. There were no cobwebs. It was very clean at Auntie Cartier's. The weather was bad all day, the Seine was disgusted, the boats and the barges all leaked water in so many places that the seamen had had it. Uncle Pierrot would meet up with them while Auntie Cartier dusted and together they'd go to the café near the square.

Even though I was quiet and unassuming, they wouldn't let me into the local pre-school where I saw kids just a little older than me, walking with their teachers in Asnières. I began to feel low for the first time in my life – I wasn't vaccinated against feeling low in 1964. What's more, since the school was near our house, if I'd been able to go there, Maman wouldn't have had to drag me, the Edgar package, above the barges moored at the quay and on strike, all the way to Auntie Cartier's place until the spring of the following year. Auntie Cartier stuffed us with slices of bread, and when her old man came out of the bedroom, we kids fought over who would bring him his slippers. Auntie was constantly cleaning the kitchen, preparing meals, and feeding us, and my cheeks and butt kept getting bigger. I could have rolled there on my own in the morning if it weren't for my ears slowing me down. Bernard didn't come to our house every evening. He often arrived when I was already in bed. He had a Simca 1000, and in the morning when he'd spent the night at our place, he dropped us at Mme. Cartier's. I liked that, crossing the bridge in a Simca. Maman smelled very nice, she always looked sharp when she went to work in the smoked-glass building behind the trees. Since it was raining, her gaze grew more and more dark and traumatized each time she turned to me. On Saturday afternoon she took me to the park in Bécon, which is also where there was the doctor for my wandering ears. I could feel there was something wrong. Some days Auntie Cartier would stop several times while doing her housework

– cleanliness is what matters most in kids' lives – and look at me. She wasn't like Mme. Clarisse Georges because her eyes were small and brown, whereas at Rue d'Avron where I was born the eyes of Mme. Clarisse Georges were still under the shock of discovery. Edgar was born. Sometimes, I wish I could remember from the beginning so I could know who my father was.

"You're not my papa," I said to Bernard.

He looked at Isabelle. She looked at him. He didn't know what to say.

"You're not my papa."

After that I was almost four, it rained like a pissing cow all the time, and Uncle Pierrot pulled on his boots to go check out the extent of the damage. The water rose to the road along the riverbank near the Hispano Suiza factory, we were all very worried about the boatmen in the café below. Uncle Pierrot was nobody's papa, I couldn't see myself spending much time with him since I was afraid of the water. But that's exactly what interested him most. He took me with him with my ears in full sail, holding my hand like my life depended on it, and we stood on the banks of the river, watching the rats. He pointed them out to me, I didn't see them all.

"You have to take Edgar outside, Madame Isabelle, we can't let him breathe all that dust, it's bad for him!

"Do you think so, Madame Cartier?"

"Of course, come now, Madame Isabelle."

So Maman bought me rubber boots, and I started to look like Uncle Pierrot except for the ears, which didn't match, and the mustache and everything else. That's what was most interesting about the end of the year 1964, awaiting the flood. We also went with Isabelle and Bernard to Ménilmontant for my birthday. Bernard didn't stay until the end, he couldn't. The place was crowded with people who wore butterfly-frame glasses, and I got nice presents, though I don't remember them. What I remember most is that Isabelle's ears were all red when she played cards, near the bottles. I was sitting on her lap, and we won. Isabelle loved to play belote, like everyone else in the neighborhood. When we went back to visit Mme. Clarisse Georges after I turned four, Maman had the same gaze as usual, only worse. Maybe I wasn't more

44

under-achieving than the national average after all, except for drawing. I really was the worst at drawing of all the kids born at the hospital at Rue d'Avron since the renovation of the maternity ward. I was so bad at it that she stopped borrowing the Caran d'Ache pencils to make them squeak. Instead, she placed cubes on the table, and I made piles according to color and numbers without screwing up. Mme. Clarisse Georges was very old in 1964, but even so she had eyes that didn't move and there was no way to escape them. Without any encouragement from Maman I lost my words. I heard her say to herself, *Edgar, make an effort, Edgar, for pity's sake* and she grimaced each time I chose the red instead of the green. As a matter of fact, Mme. Clarisse Georges's gaze was giving me a stomachache – I became Edgar-the-Runs in 1965, but we're not there yet. I still did a good job anyway.

"Edgar, tell me your name."

I wanted to bawl but I felt Isabelle losing it, so I told the psychiatrist that my name was Edgar, as if I didn't know that we were awaiting the flood of rats.

She raised her white eyebrows until they touched her

frames. Then I felt I was on the right track for someone to finally fill me in.

"Uncle Pierrot says we'll end up flooded with big rats eating our feet.

"Uncle Pierrot?"

She didn't know Uncle Pierrot either.

"I'm afraid of Uncle Pierrot's rats."

"What, sweetie? Why are you afraid of rats?"

"Because I want to go to school so I won't have to stay there waiting for the flood of rats and watching Auntie Cartier sweep up dust bunnies and dust her dolls.

As you can see, I was on a roll, and after that everything became blurred, I have gaps in my memories. I waited for Maman in the waiting room at Rue d'Avron. I played nicely with the little fatty who was there every time, she didn't even know how to say ouch when you pulled her hair. Then, we returned the way we came, Isabelle and I, by métro and the train at Saint-Lazarre. I don't remember well when I stopped going to Uncle Pierrot's, who was always watching the barges that might end up on top of the road along the bank for all we knew, with stairwell C of the building across the way, where the rats only had one floor to climb. Isabelle looked for another caregiver but with my ears and my not being all there, the ones she found were already full that year and even the next, which was approaching.

She talked about the Edgar package with Bernard too when he came over to our house.

"I don't know what to do. I can't leave him here."

Now I had doubts, and could no longer meet her gaze easily.

"You should send him to the countryside. Did you talk to the social worker? It would do him good."

"Do you think so?" Isabelle answered.

"Well, yes. It's the best solution."

"You think so?"

Our next-door neighbor looked after me for a little while. Finally, Maman took some of her vacation days and we left. I must have liked the train ride. We scarfed down sandwiches, and since the train was climbing, soon there weren't any rats to snatch the crumbs. We both slept, the trip lasted a long time. I remember that Isabelle was the most beautiful unwed mother in the entire train station at Gare de Lyon. I know this because we walked up and down the entire platform to find the right train car, which we didn't find at first because Bernard hadn't read the ticket. When I think of him now he doesn't even have eyes. Often, in my memory, I walk up the platform at Gare de Lyon, not all there, with my suitcase and Isabelle, who'd hardly spoken for days. In fact, I was leaving one giant to meet another.

The new one had come to meet us at the train station, where I was freezing my butt off it was so cold out. He was very tall too. He took the suitcase from Maman that held my things, and I didn't understand why her eyes had become all red like when we went to bed and she argued with my papa Bernard, who had an unwed mother in Levallois-Perret and a wedding band that slipped off his finger every time he washed his hands before eating. I hadn't understood that my trip would last a long time. When I came back I was eleven years old.

*

Still, it feels weird to tell you about those years. I'm not the same Edgar, obviously. And, I'd have actually preferred staying longer in 1964, and for something more interesting to have happened on the train, I'm not sure what exactly. Let's imagine the old lady from Parc Monceau had been sitting across from us with her pink hair, and my papa Bernard had taken the seat nearest the corridor. We might've never met him, Maman and I. When he stepped out into the corridor to smoke cigarettes and look at the view, I did too, I enjoyed looking. My eyes were level with the bottom of the window and *E pericoloso sporgersi. Ne pas se pencher au dehors.* Through the window was another country. Isabelle was reading Françoise Sagan with her legs crossed and her scarf tied to her wrist like she often did for travel. Maybe she'd seen it in her book. I didn't know how to read in 1964, or even the following years, because I mostly had not being all there to occupy me instead of letters. We ate on the train, Isabelle wasn't embarrassed to unwrap the tin foil, and she gave me ham sandwiches. Near Dijon, the giant stopped the bar-cart that was being pushed by a young guy with long hair that hid ears like mine. Bernard offered me a Coke. He wasn't a doctor or an accountant at Phosphatines du Nord-Est, the baby cereal company, he was just on a trip on his own. The old lady didn't faint, but she still had pink hair because of the sunset through the train window. She slept the whole time and even when the train stopped at a station, she only opened one eye because she was going to the end of the line. So Isabelle and Bernard started to talk about everything and nothing.

"My name is Bernard, Bernard Langin."

"I'm Isabelle."

I don't remember if she said Isabelle right away to Bernard or if she just listened: yes yes, because this time she wasn't afraid of being attacked by the unwed mothers at Parc Monceau. Then, on the train, we walked up and down the corridor to stretch our legs, and Bernard took me to take a piss. The ground flashed by through the hole in the toilet and it almost made me not have to go anymore. He smoked the same cigarettes as Isabelle, Craven from 1964, the packs were white and red. Then we returned to the car. She said, be good Edgar, I'll be right back.

"Don't worry, I'll take care of him."

"Thank you, sir."

"My name is Bernard."

"Thank you."

Isabelle smiled faintly, he was so eager for her to know his name, even Edgar the noodle could see that. He pulled a few sheets of paper from his bag. Since I was sitting across from the old lady, he unfolded the seat tray, which reminded me of the little Formica table in our kitchen in Asnières, at home. He took a large black marker from his pocket and handed it to me.

"Here you go, Edgar buddy, draw something for me."

I gave him my moron look from the special unit at the hospital at Rue d'Avron and he just smiled at me again.

"I'm not going to steal your mother away from you, buddy."

I agreed with that.

I pulled in my lolling tongue and started to tell the whole story. At one point, the pink-haired old lady opened a teary eye because of the pressure of her memories and glanced at the damn drawing I was making, which was so beautiful, it would've made Mme. Clarisse Georges' glasses fall off.

"We still have a ways to go, Madame, Bernard said to her. You can go back to
sleep, I'll watch your purse.

"What day is it?" asked the old lady.

"Monday."

"Monday, oh, what a pretty drawing. Is he your son?"

Bernard gave a nod and winked, and I understood, with my ears. She fell asleep again. I can't remember the drawing of 1964, though. Isabelle was looking out the window, and it must have been the most beautiful view that year, because I'd already had my birthday in Ménilmontant, though I didn't remember it well, as you know. The wind didn't muss the old lady's hair, and the trees along the highway that the train followed were all bent in the same direction.

"Done," I told my papa Bernard.

"Well, well, let me see."

He looked at the drawing and then he looked at me. "Buddy, hats off, it's not every day you see drawings like that.

"I'm not your buddy."

"Yes, Edgar, I know that. You are Edgar, the son of Isabelle. She is watching the trees speed by along the tracks and the highway, we are going very fast. Do you want to make another drawing?"

"Well yes," I said softly. "If you want one, I'll make you one."

I produced another outstanding piece, meanwhile I heard Bernard thinking with one ear.

I'm not going anywhere, I want her, she knows it, we have time. I could stay here for hours, except we're on the express. Too bad, too bad. What's that book she's reading? Françoise Sagan, I've always wondered what she could be going on about. Let's have a look.

So we stay there a little longer, I think I even make a drawing for the old lady while I'm at it, and when Isabelle sees them, she has such a shock that my ears forget to listen as she puts away her things because we're getting off soon. She's listening to Bernard, he's talking about Françoise Sagan, 1964, and how he likes her work a lot. Maman is stunned. How can he read half her thoughts and know what's in my head too, just from seeing the drawings? But we're already in the next year.

I wish I could make some years that I listen to through the others last longer and not hear the ones that are here in front of me. But even if I try very hard, I always hear in the same way. Isabelle wasn't there anymore.

UNCLE JOS AND AUNTIE GINA'S

B EFORE ME, I really wonder what there was. Kids often believe that everything begins the moment they're born, but not your humble servant Edgar. I'm not even sure I could find the place where I lived before without making a mistake, Madame Clarisse Georges. I'm still not all there, but I know how to hide it well. I'm grown up now. I'm still quiet and unassuming too, but I'm not sure that won't change. Sometimes I want to shorten all this and get right to the train station platform, to the moment we're going home. I'll be eleven then.

Eleven was a good year for me, the ones before too, and with my ears wide-open I take a deep breath and dive into the past, without remembering much actually. A long time ago, Isabelle was my maman. That I remember. Then, at eleven, I will return to school in Paris, a boarding school. I was happy before. I didn't have my papa Bernard anymore and I didn't see Isabelle much. She didn't come see me often, she didn't have the money to come. When she arrived, it was her gaze I remembered best. So there it is, the rest Edgar let run through the gaps in his mind. Auntie Gina doesn't talk to me about it, she doesn't answer the questions that the kids ask, she's like all kids' caregivers, you know. She understands the stories we tell her, illness, food, and homework. The rest, she doesn't even want to hear about. In short, if I don't remember much, Madame Clarisse Georges, I still remember some, and as soon as we see each other, I want to say to you: don't give me the Caran d'Ache pencils, I don't want to break the tips this time. I don't even want to tell you how funny you look behind your crushed-glass compound eyeglasses, Madame Georges. Make up your mind. Am I lucky to have several people acting as parents for me? If you don't want to answer, let me choose for myself, I'll back up like the tractor that belonged to old Claud whose children Marie and André were even stupider than Edgar, if you remember him. A long time ago, the midwives yelled at unwed mothers at Rue d'Avron, the windows were up high and the great room was lit with bulbs like flying saucers. Or else I'll stay with the Clauds on the tractor, even if I've never looked after cows, I can still learn, we have almost the same ears, the cows and me.

Sometimes I remember too much, you know. I'd prefer, if it's not too much trouble, not to mix up everything in my head and stay on the tractor in the summer, it's called the harvest. The harvest is dangerous because of the poisonous snakes basking in the sun. We drink and sock juice fills our boots, but that way we won't get bitten and die. I'd like to see you when I return, Madame Clarisse Georges. Auntie Gina has black eyes, black hair and beautiful arms, she's a little bit Italian, like everyone I've met since I got here, not far from Piedmont, when Isabelle and I took the train in winter. With Uncle Jos, it's different, he doesn't like Italians, even though he married one and she's not the first, but I only know that because I let my ears listen. They always hang out in the kitchen, by the oilcloth with burns and knife marks and old stains. Uncle

Jos's gaze is as blue as a sled dog's and he has road workers from the Department of Roads and Ditches who are all the time filling the holes of the world so it won't spill over on all sides. Sometimes at night he goes out in his underwear, wearing his Damart thermals, when the roads collapse and no one can get through.

I've seen his ass at night because the phone isn't in the bedroom. He goes out with his boots and all the equipment from the Department of Roads and Ditches. These days, when the kids get up in the morning, he's already dressed and calculating the bad weather and how many hours the road workers will need and whether the snow will last. The road workers drink white wine with him. I go to school. Uncle Jos smacks the kids but just when he's having a moment or if he's worked up for one reason or another, the rest of the time he's cheerful. Since you know everything, with Isabelle far away you could maybe tell her that we should wait a little longer. After all, I'd like to stay here with them, and still go to school, the one where you have to walk by the dog. I Edgar have a problem with the dog on the road. I'm still a little bit Edgar-the-Runs from time to time because of the black watchdog at the end of the chain at the Hôtel des Charmilles. But eventually us kids still manage to arrive at the public school across from the pharmacy run by Mme. Nguyen. Next to it there's L'Étoile des Alpes, where we buy candy in secret. Mme. Rizzante is friends with Auntie Gina, so we can't steal any without her finding out. To get home we go all the way back down the go-see road without stopping by the hound of Charmilles, and we get the smack of the century or the whip with the pretty colors. It has sharp ends, the lashes have little red, white, and blue tips, it bites the skin on your ass. Before, Auntie Gina walked with us along the go-see, where the Claud brothers always win the competition when we hold onto the electric fences. André doesn't have much of a brain — at Rue d'Avron, they could examine his ears like they did mine, and his nose is crooked. André is my friend. But I've never tended cows, and if I close my eyes I simply remember Isabelle's gaze, she's as afraid of dogs as I am. So I can't see her taking me to school around here, all we would do is scare ourselves to death, she and I. I don't know if you're still alive, I have to say, Madame Clarisse Georges. Here I've already seen stiffs who didn't have pink hair because they're Dutch and didn't have a license. I've grown up.

It's at the Sauvages campground, in the summer the Dutch always dive in at the same spot, where the sign with white letters on a red background says that in fact it's dangerous and drowning is forbidden. I don't quite remember when it was. Those Dutch assholes, I saw two taken away by the divers and the police, and Uncle Jos said to me, stay here, we were in the field digging potatoes. I'm going to tell you about the potatoes first, Madame Clarisse Georges, so that you don't get all your pencils mixed up, if you still want me to draw my life for you, I can speak to you now. In school, Auntie Gina always says I'm not as good for nothing as the mayor's daughter, who never showed her pussy to André Claud, who knows about agriculture like his father and has the same crooked nose, whereas my papa Bernard, even when I repeat to myself papa Bernard papa Bernard Bernard Bernard while I wait to fall asleep, I don't remember his face. All I have left is his Simca 1000. He was very tall too.

Uncle Jos and I were digging potatoes next to the big Findus warehouse on the bank of the river by the brambles. The Dutch trailer irritated Uncle Jos, who couldn't stand trailers or Dutch people or, when he was irritated, cigarette smoke or priests or rightwingers or peasants – or especially Italians from the border or the Swiss next to them. I was between his legs to pick up the pace. This time I got a heavy blow to the skull he was so worked up. He almost dug my head off. Right away I saw my life from before and the train on the bridge. After that we went with Auntie Gina who pulled me by the arm over to Mme. Nguyen. She made mixtures for virility, André had even stolen some from his father but nothing happened right away. The bandage Mme. Nguyen put on me was so large that she plastered my ear and I went back an hour later to show Uncle Jos the hole he'd made in my head. But when I saw him by the river, I thought he'd had a moment of madness as if he'd been bitten by a snake. He was coming back up, balancing on the dam, right where the water bubbled a little before it turned green further down, but it seemed almost black where the Dutch people hadn't read the sign. I saw the Dutch lady first, Madame Clarisse

Georges, she had very light eyes. From being naked so much, she was very tan, almost as though she hadn't even died that day. Uncle Jos couldn't swim.

He bought a small boat not long after that, I don't know if it was related because at first it was always at the back of the garage, where we stacked kindling. He wanted to have his small boat at Lake Annecy to piss off the fish on the right. He could have worn his straw hat to fish. He yelled for me to go back up to the house to tell Gina, I started to run, but Auntie Gina had been watching everything like Mme. Rizzante, Nadino's mother, and also Mme. Tapies, Annette's mother near the school who saw everything through the window by pulling back the drapes. We almost bumped into each other. Auntie Gina had a hand on her heart to prevent an attack, and a Virgin Mary, like yours but not hidden, I was in the middle of the field and she was running. I thought very hard of Isabelle to make her come and even my papa Bernard but I didn't succeed. Auntie Gina ran without looking at anything because Uncle Jos couldn't swim, and he didn't have the road workers from Roads and Ditches on hand to order them to obey and to look for the other Dutchman in the vicious hole in the Fier – that's the name of the river, Edgar your humble servant. He was talking to the dead woman who was naked like him when there were landslides during the night. He was going to take a piss before he intervened. Auntie Gina pulled him toward the riverbank, and she took off her shoes to climb on the dam, I don't know why Uncle Jos started to slap the Dutchwoman like he hadn't seen she was dead. Her tongue lolled, a little like Edgar, if you remember him. On the dam, Auntie Gina walked like the high-wire dancer from the Gypsy circus we would go see, the one with the donkey named Cadichon, above the pharmacy in the village field, where we also went with M. and Mme. Vidone to pick up old bones for the deputy mayor. He wasn't in the same party as Uncle Jos, but they'd have a drink together and look at the bones in a fishing crate. According to him, they were very old Ostrogoth bones we'd found and also animal bones with no history. She raced across the dam on one side, then all of a sudden, she disappeared into the black water, so I started running too like a departing train but I saw her head bob up. Soon, going very quickly along the road to the Findus warehouse, there were divers in dark blue minivans. They pulled Gina out first. She was all wet, she was breathing fast. Still, she ran toward Uncle Jos, who was already chewing out the emergency rescue for getting there after the Dutch people were already dead, because it was forbidden to die there, he'd put up that sign for a reason. It's the only time I saw them completely in each other's arms, like I have no memory even of Isabelle talking like that except when she was on the phone, it was 1970, just before the big toad in the field, because misfortune never comes alone.

I tried to go see the firemen and the policemen to tell them I'd never seen dead Dutch people since the dawn of time, but Uncle Jos started yelling at the kids to get back up the field fast. Auntie Gina crossed herself and gave me a stern look.

"Come, Edgar, don't stay there, you look like the village idiot."

She didn't go to mass much, mind you, I'm not sure she prayed with the words they taught us because she often spoke the dialect of the Dagos who'd been around since the liberation of France. As a result, I didn't know in 1970 if I was

Edgar born at Rue d'Avron or the Edgar who was a Dago like
Nadino and most of the kids at school, except the Clauds,
who were too stupid to leave the barn, and the daughter of
the rightwing mayor, who'd come from Lyon just to piss off
Uncle Jos. I'd have liked to have been someone's son that
evening, and even that whole year I didn't see Isabelle, but
she called on Sunday evenings. The phone was in the room
down the hall. I put on felt slippers to go there.

"It's Maman, Edgar. Edgar, are you well?"
It was a black telephone. Even today, despite my big ears, I
have trouble with the phone. I didn't know what to say, not
being all there. It was like I had pieces of myself everywhere,
and it'd been a long time, Madame Clarisse Georges, you can
prepare a thousand sheets of paper and all the Caran d'Ache
pencils like at the Fournier department store where we went
every September.

"Yes, goodbye." I was fed up with crying in 1970, I tried
to hold back my tears long enough for Isabelle to find something to say.

"And school, is it going well?"

"I found some more bones for the deputy mayor."

"Ah, bones. And your ears, are your ears ok?"

"Well yes."

I hadn't had ear infections in a long time. Isabelle didn't want to believe it.

"And school, is it going well?"

"Well yes."

Then Auntie Gina would come up behind me in the office where Uncle Jos drew up plans to annoy the land registry. Even for the phone Auntie Gina took off her apron. To this day, I still remember the pink-haired old lady and Gina's white and blue apron as if they could make me all there: your Edgar in two drawings, except for the rest. Isabelle sent the check in an envelope because I wasn't free in those days. It was Auntie Gina who opened it. She always put the envelope in the same place so that Edgar wouldn't see it, Uncle Jos sometimes asked her if she had received it. She looked at him with narrowed eyes and moved her lips, but Edgar the noodle dragged his ears in his soup, he didn't hear a thing.

Those times Isabelle came I didn't like it so much. Sometimes, I would've liked to pick up the phone again and tell her, like Uncle Jos did, Edgar come here. He pulled my ears and smelled of white wine. I liked it when he stank a little, waiting for coffee after a meal, before going out.

"Here's what we're going to do."

"Yes, Uncle."

"You're going to go to your mother's to study at boarding school and afterward you'll come back here. I'll show you how to handle all these Dagos and peasants, we're going to conquer all of Savoy, you and me. We'll be independent, no one left to mess with our lives.

"Yes, Uncle." Edgar bent over laughing at that one because we were going to have fun. Edgar for president.

"Stop it Jos, look at his face, he doesn't understand."

"I'll explain it to him."

Then he slid me off his knee and if it was a day he'd had white wine to drink, he'd get worked up like a maniac, especially in the evenings, after having been at work yelling at the road workers from Roads and Ditches, who were so sloshed they rolled around in them instead of filling them. If they drank too much it was because we weren't independent, according to him. What's more, apart from my repaired ears, you'll see how I've lost weight. I'm not the same Edgar as when I had a knit hat in winter, those years. I walk, I run, I kick. I never told Isabelle I didn't want to come back, I was supposed to return to see the Seine for boarding school and to gain independence, forbid the Dutch from the dam, they were dense like Edgar when I was little. When I grow up, I'll come back.

The Dutch tent stayed up for a good while by the river. In the evenings, I watched the trains. My room was big but less so than the years before. Then the police returned to remove the remains, we even had a meeting at the village hall, where Uncle Jos would take me because he hated not having kids around to stand in for the road workers. I didn't get everything because they were speaking Italian and also, here, I was with my caregiver not my maman. Sometimes the monthly payments for me were late, but I don't know if that interests you. Auntie Gina didn't tell me, but she always hid the check in the same place, she counted in a notebook, I'd learned numbers with my teacher Mme. Lydie Vidonne, who liked to pick up the deputy's bones too. I thought Isabelle was still a shorthand typist in the glass building, but in fact she'd changed jobs to start a new one called secretary. I liked the meetings in the village hall. I backed Uncle Jos, he was the head of all the kids who lived at Gina's, I'll tell you their names, Madame Clarisse Georges, in case it interests you to meet them. In the evenings, Gina was cross because Uncle Jos would take me to watch the news with him, though personally I'd have preferred slowing down my ears and going to sleep, I even watched movies about the Second World War, like the Battle of Stalingrad, where millions of Russians were killed to save Edgar and his ears, exactly like in Savoy, which was stolen by the French. Uncle Jos had fits in front of the black-and-white TV.

"Let it be a lesson! Don't fall asleep Edgar, for God's sake! Look! Look!"

I was going to go back to Paris by train to take care of the problem of the century, Edgar for president, Savoy and the Bretons, they were making babies behind our backs, buckets of unwed mothers. With him to handle the land registry and the road workers we would start a revolution for sure when I grew up, and we would show them. I don't want to go into all the details, Madame Clarisse Georges, in case you're a Breton or a Dago, but I would like to talk to someone. If you're not dead, I wouldn't mind if it were you. I look into your eyes, and I search for Isabelle.

*

In any case Edgar has made a lot of progress since 1964, I can't imagine anyone who'd say otherwise. When we see each other, I'll draw the big toad for you too, because we didn't have the rats there like when I was little. It was in the brush, one day Uncle Jos was cutting with the sickle and I was behind him making a stack with the rake when we saw an enormous toad. He missed his shot, and the toad squirted from everywhere.

"Goddammit! Holy shit!"

He rushed backwards. I heard the explosion. The toad went up in a geyser of white and green shit like the juice of a hundred million dandelions. Edgar again had the scare of the century in 1970, Uncle Jos screamed again.

"Goddammit! What is that thing?"

Even the deputy didn't know. It wasn't listed in his books.

We set it on fire, Edgar the pyromaniac, like we did to slugs too, in a big wash-boiler. We'd boil them, and the kids would get an earful, at first the slugs would try to climb up the sides of the boiler, and they'd cry, us kids had a long stick to push them back down, and they fried while saying their prayers. The following day they were stuck to the sides. In 1970, Edgar has so many things to remember that you understand why I wouldn't want to come home. I'm scared that my being not all there will start acting up again when I'm far from here. Isabelle calls me on Sunday nights, and she asks:

"Edgar, are you well?"

I try to tell her about it, but I can't. Instead, I talk to her about the toad, in case she's interested. On the phone, I hear as if it's next door. I also hear Maman asking herself things, I don't know what, I hear her dark and traumatized gaze because it's the same one she has when she comes down here for a Sunday visit. It's heavy to my eyes. Uncle Jos often goes to pick her up at the station on his own, meanwhile Auntie Gina scrubs me, because it's the inspection of Edgar when she comes. I still have my floppy ears with stuff in them, and she looks in my underwear, I don't wipe well.

71

"And is school going well?"

"Well yes."

I don't know what else to say after yes. In the evening, when I hang up the phone, I want to talk to Gina. I want her to hug me, to hold me in her arms. I see the Paris train go by, always at the same time, over the new bridge that's above the old one, and even further above the very old footbridge, not even a bicycle bridge, where even the Dutch don't go because it dates from before me. Even Gina and Uncle Jos weren't born, and Uncle Jos seems old to me. Then, once the train has gone by, I sleep, I have a hot brick rolled up in an old sheet and I put it under my stomach. I'm nice and warm. I put on my winter cap like Uncle Jos at night, whose ass is bare but everything else is in Damart thermals. Sometimes, I try to remember before. I hear pieces, I only have pieces that don't stick. For the rest, when I open my ears to the max, all I hear are the slugs, the toads exploding, the water running under the dam, the deputy's bones, Mme. Lydie Vidonne's dictations, Maman's silence when she listens to what I don't even tell her, maybe she wouldn't want to know. I'm still the same Edgar, after all, I tell myself, I got the Caran d'Ache pencils that we went to buy at Fournier's, these are the drawings I made, if I'm allowed to bring them in my suitcase, you'll see how I remember, Madame Clarisse Georges, with you I wouldn't mind.

Instead, I dream of trains. Or else of Isabelle. I hear so well with my big flaps that I could call out the pages of her book. She turns them. It's evening. Often, at night, she keeps leaving and returning, and I don't know what way she's going, if it's the Gare de Lyon or the cold train station where Uncle Jos refuses to go beyond the lines of taxis because of the city he doesn't like. I remember today that I've never heard Uncle Jos say anything in secret. Sometimes, the kids hear Gina and him making love, but I couldn't swear to it on the Italian flag, all I ever saw was his ass coming out of the Damart thermals. He believed that death lurked at every orifice, he was in a war of attrition with cold drafts. I liked that.

"Edgar, open the door, close the window, no, not too wide, there, open the basement window, go up to the bedrooms, there's a window open. Man digs his grave with his teeth!"

The shutters bang, I'm afraid to close the shutters, because of the trains going by, Auntie Gina too is afraid of the north wind. Outside, she places her closed fists on her heart where she thinks it will hit, the wind, I do the same. To go to the doctor when I was still sick, we took the bus. I don't even move my knee when he gives me a little tap with his hammer, but I'm always moving around in my head, where I wait for Isabelle. I remember her name and also her gaze, but I'm not old enough yet to love only the eyes, you know. After school, Auntie Gina does the dishes. We kids are lined up at the table with newspapers so we won't get the wax cloth dirty, and we do our homework, and then drawings. I'm still the worst at drawings. Mind you, I read the newspaper underneath, it's called *L'Huma des dimanches* or sometimes *Réveillez-vous* which says that the end of the world is coming, according to information read in the stars and other things, like smoke and white wine, man digs his grave with his teeth! Us kids we like the end of the world: it scares us shitless. I don't want to tell you about the kids I was with because some years they changed often and others they stayed. We're together all the time. Auntie Gina moves between the chairs, I'm the village idiot, but when I come back from boarding school, I'll have done the studies of the century to stop the end of the world and fix the boiler. I'll be the president. I was ok with it, mind you, except for the boiler. I didn't like going down to the boiler so much. As much as we all fought to be first with Uncle Jos's slippers and to pull off his road workers' boots from Roads and Ditches, I still didn't like going down to the basement with him. In the summer, he also made soft water for a better life for all, and we had to go downstairs again in the evening to add the big white balls to the Culligan water softener.

"Man digs his grave with his teeth! Goddammit!"

At the boiler, we always had the fright of our lives when he opened the little door to show us the flames of the roaring inferno, and you could climb into it, even if I had a big Down head. I still preferred the water softener and the large stinky balls in light blue plastic bags, like the water in the new crapper at the community room, where they have parties. With M. Vidonne, we also went skiing on Children's Day, it's good for us. Isabelle had bought me Rossignol skis the year of the revolution in Paris that wasn't a part of Uncle Jos's plan. We all went together on the bus.

Sometimes, Madame Clarisse Georges, I grew up very fast and other times it's as if I were still on the go-see road in front of the stupid black watchdog. I've never been inside the Hôtel des Charmilles, where there was never anyone except that dog drooling in front of its bowl and baring its teeth. Usually, Auntie Gina watched us from the kitchen window all the way as far as she could see, then it was Nadino's mother, so we couldn't do anything truly dumb. Only one day when there was the revolution in Paris, I don't know what came over me, I was having a serious problem with the dog, because every time we walked by he was there guarding his bowl with his look of rage. I wanted to find out what he ate that gave him that mean look. For us Thursdays, for example, was polenta, which is eaten by chewing because otherwise you can't shit it out until some time in the hazy future, it's so heavy. I'm afraid of dogs, but I moved forward anyway. He was sitting on his front paws with his ass up in the air as though he knew Edgar's belly was heavy with polenta. Hôtel des Charmilles hadn't been repainted since the dawn of time, and the vines of the arbor wall fell down like the ropes of old pirates who had left in a hurry, I approached very slowly.

Then he took off after me like a maniac and I had the runs of the century because he bit me on the leg. I still have the scar, if you want to look. I always wore long pants so the dog only tore off half the pant leg, and then there was no one at the hotel. The Charmilles was just for cold drafts and the poor guys getting cheated on who parked further up behind Étoile des Alpes. My teacher Mme. Lydie Vidonne disinfected my wound. The kids came home from school, and Auntie Gina was waiting for me with the whip, the one Uncle Jos had cut the lashes on, what's more I'd had the runs on the way home from school by the go-see road – though by now the dog didn't give a damn about Edgar, he wasn't all there either, he was old, with ears like wet rags, and barked only when we'd already passed by. My velvet pants were torn, I had the runs. I don't know what else of importance happened other than that, the weather was nice when we came home from school.

"You smell bad, Edgar," Gina said to me.

"I didn't do it on purpose, Auntie."

"Your pants are torn!"

"I didn't do it on purpose!"

She told the kids to open the gate and filled a washtub with water, I had to wash my butt in the tub right in the middle of the courtyard, so everyone knew all the way to Geneva that Edgar had it all over him. I bawled like a calf, then I went to empty the tub. Gina had never done that to me before. That evening we finished the polenta, and Uncle Jos didn't enlist me to go watch TV because there was nothing good on: things were really blowing up in Paris.

*

Mme. Lydie Vidonne was my favorite teacher, besides, I didn't have any others. I liked going to school because we had nature class and skiing, we picked up bones, and learned numbers and grammar. Sometimes, when I was talking with the kids, I told them I came from the hospital at Rue d'Avron and that I climbed the Eiffel Tower, just to mess with them, except it didn't even bother them. I was only on loan at Uncle Jos and Auntie Gina's, there were the envelopes from Isabelle that she always put in the same place behind the vase on the buffet where we kept the plates and glasses. Especially since maybe we hadn't been to the Eiffel Tower, the kids said I was lying, and I told them about Parc Monceau, which is the most beautiful place on Earth, where I went with my baby-roller and my papa Bernard the chief accountant, but I wasn't sure I remembered it anyway. I only had Isabelle and I wasn't all there, after all.

I was always quiet and unassuming in nature class, Mme. Lydie Vidonne was short, she wore flowered skirts, she was friends with Mme. Nguyen from the pharmacy where it cost an arm and a leg. Nadino told us about her pussy because he'd compared hers with his cousin's, he could see everything through her skirt. I was angry with Auntie Gina, and the next day when we went out with the kids on the go-see road, Edgar was the only one in shorts. In fact if my ears could hear even deeper than they already do, I'd wonder if it wasn't the oversee, or else the sightsee road, I don't know which is the best of the three. I stayed without saying anything all day running things around in my bean. I was next to Nadino, who was a redhead, and his father had a white van marked Rizzante, which is why I even know how to write their name.

"Edgar, stay there," said the teacher.

The kids went to play Jailbreak in the schoolyard, right across from Mme. Nguyen's pharmacy.

"Edgar, what's the matter?"

I tried to give her my moron look but I'd forgotten how to do it, so I told Mme. Lydie Vidonne that I didn't have a papa and that the kids didn't believe that I had seen the Eiffel Tower when I was little. I also said that they'd never seen my maman Isabelle in the flesh, they didn't believe she existed either. There weren't color photos yet. Once again, I did the stupidest thing of the century that year, but Madame Clarisse Georges, it must be said that I was going to save the kingdom of Savoy and take the place of the mayor who'd come from Lyon, where there's smoke, there's fire. I would have traded Maman for Mme. Lydie Vidonne too, sometimes. I liked her flowered skirts, she never yelled, and she smelled almost the same as Isabelle. She knew all kinds of things too, Mme. Vidonne, she talked softly on purpose so the kids would hear pins drop, but I always listened carefully with her. She nodded.

"And Uncle Jos, Auntie Gina, all's well?"

"Well yes," I answered.

"Go on Edgar, go play in the yard with the others."

She must have written to Isabelle, because in 1968, I received a letter. Uncle Jos had sent me to fetch it because we also fought among us kids to fetch the mail. As a result, we each had a turn. There were a lot of us at that time, because of the unwed-mothers revolution. I was already the one who'd been there the longest since I was almost eight. Isabelle wrote with a black felt-tipped pen, we had inkwells on the desks, Auntie Gina had a blue or black Bic ballpoint for her crosswords after lunch. Uncle Jos was always looking for his glasses, so I don't remember for him. Isabelle, Isabelle. Sweetie, and school, is it going well? Afterward, that's when I learned that I didn't really have a papa, now that I had reached the age of reason. Hugs and kisses. I will come see you soon. See you soon, sweetheart. All right, I'd never heard of the age of reason, what I mean is, the age of reason, Madame Clarisse Georges, what was that?

I didn't go to school that afternoon. Auntie Gina was shelling beans, next to the second house that was done being built, there was a garage full of beans to be shelled, they'd been there since the year before, and even before, when Edgar, your humble servant, shelled beans with the others. Ever since the garage became a vegetable garden because we hid the beans in the soil to go faster, Auntie Gina made me come in before the kids, and I waited with her by the kitchen window, I knew all about the end of the world and also *La Vie ouvrière,* without forgetting the Larousse dictionary, which goes to show that Edgar was ready for. . . I don't know what. Uncle Jos returned from a landslide with shit up to the top of his boots. He was in a good mood. He was singing. Even now, when I think of Uncle Jos, I remember his favorite song, *avanti popolo, bandiera rossaaa!* – I need it to continue with my ears and it gives you courage, Madame from Rue d'Avron, because if you're still there, I'm not about to let you clean your glasses, on Edgar's word. I don't know why I hadn't been to school since saying those fibs to Mme. Lydie Vidonne. The evening after, Auntie Gina made me a draft for Isabelle and I copied everything neatly, school's going well, my ears are fine, Uncle Jos is well, Auntie Gina is well, the children are well, sending a heartfelt hug. I cried on the Sunday edition of *L'Huma des dimanches* because she made me start over because of the mistakes and the fingermarks. Being not all there, I'm a frustrated lefty too. And then, on Edgar's word, I'd copied everything neatly, I don't really remember how long after, but I was scrubbed with emery, it was an excellent Sunday, even Uncle Jos had a bath. We have time, Madame Clarisse Georges, so I'll first tell you about the bath.

In general, he didn't much like to have them because of the end of the world, even with the water softener, he felt there were risks. He took his bath from top to bottom, checking every draft, and for the private parts like his butt he went to the bathroom upstairs, with a boxer's robe and a wool bonnet. Us kids, we loved it when Uncle Jos had his bath. We shuttled back and forth with the towels and the Damart thermals. Uncle Jos had been the father of so many kids that he didn't give a damn anymore, he would've happily had ten more, there's so many drafts over there and work in the garden and the fields. He sang in the bathtub, *bandiera rossaaaa!* Auntie Gina boiled water in a big stewing pot in case there wasn't enough. He came out and came back head to toe in Damart underwear, the kids went out into the courtyard as

83

lookouts so people wouldn't see him in that state. Sometimes road workers appeared unexpectedly to show him some papers because they couldn't read. In the kitchen, he was all red when he came down. He brushed his teeth. Gina turned off the gas under the pot, and we went to fetch kindling to warm towels on the stove. Those were really good times, when he had his bath. As for his teeth, he was a little scary because he bled a lot, we just pretended in the evening so we could scarf down a little Colgate, but not him. After, to cauterize, he drank Calva. I think Uncle Jos liked me, Madame Clarisse Georges, he would've always needed Edgar to bring him towels, watch for drafts, and the rest obviously. We were both scrubbed with soft Culligan water, we took his Citroën DS to the train station.

"Where're we going?"

"*Avanti popolo! Bandiera rossaaaa!*"

That made Edgar laugh.

"Don't mess up my car seats, or I'll pull off your ears. We're going to pick up your mother."

I had to close my eyes because we were almost late because of the bath. It was the first time I'd gone to the train station in a long time. Isabelle was coming. I would show her off to the kids, and we would go back and forth on the go-see road, she and I, to show it was true one hundred percent. The train hadn't pulled into the station yet. But Uncle Jos was already super annoyed because of the parking spots that were paid parking now, since the change in the majority.

*

Maman you know I didn't have a chance to recognize her before she took me in her arms, because she had come first, she hadn't hesitated. I didn't right away place her dark and traumatized gaze, it wasn't like Gina's. In real life Isabelle smelled better than Mme. Nguyen and Mme. Lydie Vidonne. Uncle Jos took her little gray suitcase with the tag tied to the handle and he shook her hand as if she were a road worker, where she had a new big blue ring that really surprised me.

"Hello, Edgar, are you well?"

"Well yes."

After that, the two of us had the day of the century in 1968, when we arrived at Uncle Jos and Auntie Gina's, she didn't even think to check my ears and my butt, which shows nothing was going as planned. Auntie Gina burned the tarts and didn't have time to take off her apron, the blue one with the white flowers, she had two in all. The children of Uncle Jos, whose hair was all white now, were also at the house, it made me remember some things because we found ourselves, the two of us, in front of the steps that gave me the runs when the social worker had found the godsend for me at Uncle Jos's and Auntie Gina's in 1964. On the way back from the train station I was in the back of the car, I even found it nice, when we came the first time Uncle Jos still had an old Panhard. I felt right away how Isabelle needed me to step into the kitchen. The gravel moved under her feet and Uncle Jos who was still in a bad mood went off immediately to the garden to finish mowing.

I don't remember who took whose hand, if it was Edgar who was shy or Isabelle, but in the end we did manage to go into the kitchen. Auntie Gina hugged her, hello Madame, did you have a good trip? Isabelle who I was looking at closely said yes thank you, Auntie Gina, then she turned to me. The noise of the mower stopped, now Uncle Jos must have been behind the door taking off his boots by himself and I thought it wouldn't be a good idea to go to him. Auntie Gina brought him his nice black Sunday shoes. The other kids were outside playing in the field. Isabelle was wearing a light blue skirt and a blouse of the same color, it must have been a new thing because in the days when I went to Auntie Cartier, all her clothes were navy blue. She must have chosen light blue to go with spring and the revolution, we found ourselves seated the two of us next to each other.

Maman immediately crossed her legs. I couldn't hear anything anymore now that she was here. I would have liked it if this time she'd checked me to see how clean I was and how I had changed, I was nothing less than the new revolutionary Edgar. Besides, Auntie Gina, who was smiling at me with her eyes too, had gone all out when she'd pulled off her apron, except she was still wearing black, because of all the Italian deaths since the birth of the dawn of time. Lots of people stopped by that day, on Edgar's word. Gina started pouring drinks for everyone in the morning, Muscat, except Uncle Jos, who only drank Apremont because of the diseases of the end of the world. Isabelle said almost nothing, she let go of my hand, we looked at each other sideways because we didn't know each other as well as before, when I was little. Everyone was chatting, there were a lot of people. Ricardo had come too, and all of a sudden I understood why Uncle Jos was angry, on top of everything else. Maman had been a little scared in the car, hanging on to her handbag, I remembered her little black bag with the gold clasp perfectly, he drove like a Dago. She didn't know like Edgar did that it wasn't her fault if Uncle Jos was in a bad mood, but Ricardo's who was in the party of the outgoing mayor and his son who'd married an Italian like Auntie Gina who wasn't his mother either. Auntie Gina was bustling about at the stove, she wanted to make more tarts. At the same time Ricardo who had a Mercedes to piss off Uncle Jos' political party was talking to Maman, her voice was strange to my ears. She said words to him that I'd never heard and yes, yes, absolutely, clearing her throat from time to time, certainly, ah really, oh yes? But she'd already let go of my hand so I can't tell you why.

88

At some point, I went to the bathroom at the end of the hall that the kids had polished with bee's wax the day before by pulling each other two at a time in their slippers, and I made the most of being on the toilet to have a good cry, on Edgar's word, in case Isabelle could hear at a distance. I even wanted to take a shit just in case, but no. She still had the same gaze because when I washed my hands you should've seen my face, it's Maman I said to myself, shit, it's my maman, Isabelle, then I opened the door. I heard the rattle of everyone's words at the same time in the kitchen, Edgar still had droopy ears, I waited a good while. I don't know if you can see that with your sharp eyes, Madame Clarisse Georges, but before the meal I was still undecided. Auntie Gina was talking with Isabelle, I was behind the door. And is school going well? Auntie Gina answered yes, but you do still have to push him to do his homework, Maman answered ah, I would like to see the teacher, Auntie Gina. And then my health? It's good, answered Gina, it was better every day since my birth at Rue d'Avron, it shows how the fresh air of the mountains and a simple life, Madame Isabelle, yes, certainly, Auntie Gina, that's true, you're right. I thought again about my age, which was the same since I received the letter, and I went back to the bathroom. I don't know if I stayed there long but finally Isabelle came to get me, I was fully dressed sitting on the toilet, like on Thursdays when we had polenta. All the kids lined up to go to the toilet because sometimes Auntie Gina was so fed up she had to surrender like at Stalingrad.

About halfway down the hall there was a big mirror from floor to ceiling, Uncle Jos had bought it from peasants who were as dumb as their cows. He sometimes went to look at himself in it before going off to have a shouting match with the mayor who came from Lyon and his son the millionaire. Us kids, we'd laugh while striking poses for when we'd be independent, with Edgar chief of French Savoy. Isabelle held on to her handbag as though she still believed we would be going for a walk in Parc Monceau, she pulled from it a hand-kerchief to wipe me off, then she stood with me in front of the glass, and I saw my face with hers. I had grown a lot next to her, really a lot. Even so I still had my droopy ears, my shoes were well shined, but she looked at them longer than at Edgar. I can't remember at all what we said to each other at that moment, maybe nothing. As hard as I try, sometimes I'm even less there than usual, and even in mirrors, Edgar doesn't see anything anymore.

"You're not happy to see me, is that it?"

"Well no I am," I answered.

Isabelle bent down toward me:

"Edgar, why are you crying?"

As if I knew. I cried twice as hard, then I calmed down, we went back out together. Auntie Gina quickly pulled a cardigan on me to show Isabelle how she could be sure about my good health with her, we took a stroll in the garden, which is called taking a tour of the property.

Uncle Jos was still watering, with two or three kids to pull the hose from its reel under the bees' big linden tree, I would've liked to be with them. Over there you can water every day, even Sunday, because softened water doesn't get you dirty, or plants either. Isabelle smiled at the kids, hello, hello, hello, Renata, whose unwed mother was in Saint-Étienne came over to touch her dress, and then Renata hugged Maman.

I remember Renata well because she showed her pussy to Nadino, she had a tiny bit of pubic hair but blond. Isabelle bent toward her when she touched her dress, who are you? Maman smiled at her, I'd have liked it to be me facing her, and she answered:

"I'm Edgar's maman."

"You're pretty," Renata said to her.

Renata, Madame Clarisse Georges, you should see her too, she had a little bit of an overbite, she was like a lot of Italians at school and she wore white underwear. When there was piss, Gina left her bare-assed in the courtyard to teach her to dry herself.

"My maman is in Saint-Étienne."

Isabelle repeated, Saint-Étienne? And when Renata asked her if she paid for me monthly so she could turn tricks in peace, I was so afraid it might be true, on Edgar's word, yet I'm the quiet and unassuming kid even when it's the revolution so I went to help the others unroll the hose to make Uncle Jos happy. Ricardo wanted to stay and eat only if his wife Anita from Turino Italia could stay and eat too. Uncle Jos wasted ten times too much water, he was so fed up with the Dagos in his house. Isabelle took a walk in the garden, I showed her with all my strength how well I could unroll the hose. Now I was no longer a gift package, Madame Clarisse Georges, and when I was in the bathroom she told Auntie Gina that I looked well, except of course for my gaze and my Down face, but he got that from his father's side, I imagine, Madame Isabelle. After that I don't know the rest because I went back to the bathroom to change the subject.

We ate in the large dining room where Edgar and Uncle Jos could watch the fall of the Third Reich thanks to the party of Stalingrad. Auntie Gina kept shuttling back and forth between Uncle Jos's children. Toward the end of the meal, Ricardo lit a cigar from Havana and his father opened the windows, grumbling loudly. I don't really remember the big spread well. I was at the small table with the kids, Renata, Jean-Claude, Marie, the daughters of Ricardo and Anita, the kids of Bébert from Meythet, I showed them Isabelle. Now they knew for sure I had seen the Eiffel tower when I was little. Ricardo asked Maman for news from Paris. Actually, it really interested Uncle Jos, even though he didn't show it, because he wanted to know if they were going to blow up the Renault factory for him.

Maman had kept her handbag on her lap, put down your things, Madame Isabelle, ah yes, thank you, I would've liked to remember what she put in it. Each time she turned her eyes toward me I lifted my elbows off the table, with my head held back my ears didn't drag in the sauce, only Maman couldn't see me much because she was telling Ricardo about Paris. I would've liked to tell the kids too, in 1968 that I remembered you, Rue d'Avron, and Auntie Cartier who hated dust, and my house in Asnières, which was very big for a one-bedroom. The telephone was gray, my maman worked in an office made of smoked glass like the windows of Ricardo's Mercedes. In truth, all us kids were doing was cleaning our plates because it was nothing but stuff that was good to eat, no polenta. I remember the whole menu that day, the potatoes were tiny, Gina didn't even have time to put her apron back on. Afterward, Uncle Jos stayed alone in the dining room to fight comfortably with his son, he was making plans to mess with the land registrar and he wasn't supposed to, Ricardo was designing architects' houses. They also fought about the Algerian war. I'd often heard the story since being here. Uncle Jos had tried to break Ricardo's leg so he wouldn't go back and help the French get killed over there in the colonies, but his leg had held up against the hammer blows, so Ricardo returned to Algeria covered in gauze and bandages. Since then, the two of them didn't talk much. Me, if we had to go to war for independence, I think I'd go see Ricardo, not Uncle Jos. It feels weird, Madame Clarisse Georges, I'll always know more about Uncle Jos and Auntie Gina than about Edgar and Isabelle, and all the rest. But today, in case you're still alive and don't mind listening to me, I'm like a separated Edgar, I've already lived a long time. Before going to see my teacher Mme. Lydie Vidonne, we all went together, the kids, Isabelle and me and Auntie Gina, to the go-see road. We were the only ones who used it. Anyway it was planned ahead, that's the day I rode a bike for the first time.

Since I was still not all there, I had a hard time bicycling too. That's why Uncle Jos would make me president of Savoy and not Roads and Ditches, he said it was best to have something in your head when you didn't have a brain. The go-see road, apart from the cuckolds' dog's Hôtel des Charmilles, was bordered by the Clauds' field. We'd eaten so much, us kids, that we pushed the bike most of the way, I didn't always manage to turn the pedals, so it didn't bother me, Uncle Jos didn't come with us. He always said Edgar wants to do well, but it's no use, no way, he can't do it, for God's sake! Even though I'm quiet and unassuming, it sometimes gave me a stomach-ache because it was true, like the time he almost dug into my head when we were digging potatoes, holy fucking shit! He had a large droplet at the tip of his nose when he worked in the fields, you could see sweat around his blue eyes and in his white hair. I had Carla's bike, she was the youngest of Auntie Gina's daughters, and in those days Uncle Jos smacked her on Sunday mornings when she came home late on Saturdays. She worked in the department of Social Security and drove a midnight-blue Citroën 2CV and would take Auntie Gina and the kids to Fournier, when it was back-to-school. The bike was too big for me, I'd noticed that Isabelle didn't have much to eat. Uncle Jos got a little worked up over the French president, but Auntie Gina looked at him with her stern eyes.

So he decided to get into a fight with his son the millionaire, who was always up for it as soon as he parked the Mercedes in the courtyard, kicking up as much dust as he could.

The kids wanted to race on the go-see road. Auntie Gina and Isabelle walked behind us, Isabelle wore a little black cardigan with a big brooch on it, she gave the signal to go. Jean-Claude, who was the best at bicycling of all the kids, helped me push the pedals, but by the time he got to where I was, I'd already crashed. I got back on all by myself, Isabelle was right behind, her eyes dark and as you know I felt them behind my back. Edgar took off again, all the kids had gone past me but I was still pedaling. The go-see road is very long, at one point as Isabelle was picking poppy flowers along the Clauds' field, I turned back toward her, Maman seemed happy in the field. She wasn't watching me more than before anyway, and on the other side toward the end of La Balme, where we played with the electric wires, the kids were already at the stream where we picked watercress. All the kids ate it, until Uncle Jos learned at a party meeting that the people who owned the château and the Clauds's field were dumping all their shit into the stream, with a concrete pipe to show whose it was. My knees were all gray, and bloody. I bawled, not too loud at first, Jean-Claude came rushing back at full speed on the go-see road, which was full of dust, you had to ride in the tractors' tire tracks.

Auntie Gina liked to pick flowers too, she put them up to dry next to the envelopes and the novels she read at night. There were some by Mme. Françoise Sagan, I don't know if that was because of Isabelle, but she also read others in Italian, which is like Dago only with more *a*'s, *i*'s, and *o*'s. Jean-Claude didn't stop, he was older than me. He told me to wait, and since Isabelle had a whole bouquet of flowers, I tried again to get back on my bike, but I missed the tractor marks because I wasn't pushing hard enough and I crashed again. I really was not at all there. I remembered a lot of things about my maman at that moment, Madame Clarisse Georges, things like you, the Parc Monceau, and my arrival here. Gina looked up and to show how well she cared for Edgar, she laughed with Isabelle. Maman looked at me, her gaze darker and sadder I thought, from a distance, as she came out of the edge of the poppy field. Auntie Gina gave me the handkerchief she held in the sleeve of her blouse. Isabelle arrived with her poppies.

"Are you all right Edgar?"

"Well yes."

"It's nothing," said Auntie Gina. "He has a hard time bicycling, Madame Isabelle, let's hope that for the rest. . ."

"Let's hope so, Auntie Gina."

Then the kids all came back, because in the countess's stream there were frogs, like in the restaurants in Paris, they wanted to know if that was true too. Renata asked her do you eat frogs in Paris? She answered her no, we eat frogs' legs, not whole frogs, so the kids thought I had lied, even though it was written in black and white in *La Vie ouvrière* that Uncle Jos subscribed to, how to prepare frogs. Personally, Madame Clarisse Georges, a little after Maman's visit if you had asked for my opinion I would have liked to return to Rue d'Avron to start all over from the beginning, I think that's why I was remembering you. Isabelle pushed me a little on my bicycle while all the kids went back to look at the frogs. She was irritated that I still couldn't pedal. So I don't know how I took off on my own, Auntie Gina was looking at me strange too. For her, a kid who didn't know how to bicycle at seven was nothing but the village idiot, unless I became president of Savoy after boarding school, when I grow up. By following the track carefully, I rode to the end, Maman was carrying the flowers in the go-see road as if she were walking alone on a new street where she didn't have to go to work. When she was pushing me, I'd felt how much it bored her, I wasn't the same Edgar now. Her ears were all red and she had hay fever, me I was from the country, I wanted to be like Uncle Jos.

Auntie Gina glared at us with angry eyes when we tried to pick watercress for the anchovy salad. At the far end of the go-see road, there's a short road that cuts across the parcels of land further down, but I've never been there. Nothing changes, mind you. Isabelle and Auntie Gina seemed to get along well. They talked the whole way. We pushed our bikes until we arrived in Mme. Nguyen's courtyard, the kids asked Auntie Gina if we could go home with Uncle Jos to sit in the Dagos' Mercedes. Gina said yes, but be careful crossing the road, even if, I swear on my mother's life, no one's ever seen a car on the go-see road. Gina followed them with her eyes. See, they have a nice time here, Madame Isabelle, yes Auntie Gina. I propped Carla's bike against Mme. Nguyen's wall, where the Charmilles cuckholds parked who made Uncle Jos laugh, but when he talked about it Auntie Gina made the sign of the cross on her forehead in case she one day recognized the cars when she went to get bread at Étoile des Alpes. She also made a cross on the bread before cutting it for us to eat. There was a red animal on that wall, its name was Petrofina, but with an *o*, an *i*, and an *a*, it had nothing to do with Mme. Nguyen, on Edgar's word. Maman held my hand to cross the road.

*

I wanted to show her my whole school, which was very beautiful and would be called Stalingrad when I was president, after boarding school, and Uncle Jos would get me elected. Isabelle's hands were cold. Maybe my papa was a Dago? Then we arrived at my teacher's, who has always been my favorite teacher because she was the only one at the school. Her husband was in charge of soccer with her, I was the U10-U11 substitute, and he carted the trowels around in his car when we went to unearth the deputy's bones. He arranged them with the help of a big book to try to make a complete cadaver out of them. Isabelle put Edgar on her lap, but she couldn't see much over my ears, so Mme. Lydie Vidonne told me, Edgar, go get your notebook to show it to your maman.

"Both of them?"

"Yes, Edgar. I would also like to see your drawings."

And then she saw how Edgar was going to be the president, except for the daughter of the mayor who came from Lyon who doesn't count because she was in the wrong majority. Then Isabelle looked at my drawings, I don't remember which ones, in any case I had "good" and "very good" written on them in colored pencil or even in HB pencil. Isabelle was happy, she turned to Auntie Gina, and Mme. Lydie Vidonne, who had made tea in the school kettle, smiled. Edgar was thriving.

Then I had to go out into the courtyard, from the green gate I kept an eye on my green bicycle too, I wanted it to last. It was really a good day. Maman was happy with the poppies. Mme. Nguyen came out in her white lab coat and she waved to me lightly, with her rings on her fingers and her magic potions that she made so that people would screw her anyway, it's André who had stolen them from his father.

"Hello Madame Nguyen."

"What are you doing here, Edgar?"

"I came to see the teacher with my maman."

"Your maman? Is your maman here?"

"Yes, her name is Isabelle, Madame Nguyen."

"Say hello to Auntie Gina and your maman for me. She brought her potted plants inside to take cuttings."

Sometimes, Madame Clarisse Georges, I have strange shivers. I don't quite know how to explain it to you. I heard Isabelle talking with Mme. Lydie Vidonne, the schoolyard was empty, and I could hear everything. I played Jailbreak by myself. With the kids, I wasn't too keen on being prisoner. But that day, the ball always missed me. I thought to myself that I could escape anytime I wanted. And then, later, my bicycle started to roll on its own and it went to wait for me at the entrance, by the little door to the schoolyard. The big one was kept closed because of the neighborhood thieves, except when Monsieur Vidonne took out his Renault 4L. Then, all of a sudden, that was it, I couldn't hear anything anymore, Maman had me step outside, I didn't have good grades in drawing. I was still Edgar the noodle in 1968, and if it went on like that when I grew up I would be the chief of nothing. But I'm sorry to lie to you sometimes, on Edgar's word. Even Mme. Nguyen could explain it to you because nobody talked to her around there, except old people when they were sick and Auntie Gina, because she kept an eye on the kids instead of Nadino's maman when she made hay.

I left by myself on the go-see road. I caught a glimpse of Isabelle, and to make sure I secretly went to look through the classroom window.

Her legs were crossed, the handbag on top, the bouquet of poppies was resting on the desk. My maman, Isabelle.

"Edgar asks a lot of questions, he wants to know who his father is."

"I wrote a letter to him about it, as you recommended."

"Yes, he is a quiet, unassuming child, don't worry too much. May I ask where his father is?"

"I have no idea. Well. . . There's no chance Edgar will see him where he is. And in any case, I am divorced."

"Yes, I understand. Well, don't worry too much."

I took straight off on the go-see road on Carla's bike, in case Uncle Jos needed us, or Ricardo agreed to take us for a spin in the Mercedes. Uncle Jos was by himself mending in the field, Ricardo had left, but Anita had stayed behind with her Fiat, her daughters Cathia and Christina, and the tribe of Bébert from Meythet, who got a job with Roads and Ditches thanks to Uncle Jos, with the long arm he had in his majority. I went to Uncle Jos right away because I wanted to know if it was bad that I had a papa locked up and that I would never see him. Even with my big ears, Madame Clarisse Georges, I'd never heard it said before. He was repairing the sulfur sprayer for potato disease, for the ones below, by the river. I parked the bike, the kids were playing Battle of Stalingrad next to the woods where we get to look at Renata's pussy when we win. André taught it to us, except Stalingrad, Edgar picked the name. But I didn't feel like playing. I went over to Uncle Jos, he still had eyes more blue than yours, a runny nose beneath his beret, you can go see him too, if you like.

"And your mother, where is she?"

"With Auntie Gina."

"Well. Anyway. There's work to do. Go unroll the hose."

"Yes, Uncle Jos."

There it is. It was already the end of the revolution of 1968 for Edgar. The trains still ran, and my maman had come back on purpose to see me. While I pulled the hose, Uncle Jos went off to prune the privet hedge by the road, it had grown a lot since I'd arrived. He didn't want people to look in other people's homes and see if I'm not over there. After that, I rolled up the hose and waited for him to tell me I was free to go play with the kids. Renata had already gone off to find my maman, given that she missed hers in Saint-Étienne, which is a city of unwed mothers that's not part of Savoy. Isabelle took her hand and came over to see me, the three of us sat in the field, right across from the Brogny Bridge where the trains don't stop, except the yellow and red Micheline train with the flashing light, to look at the river below. No matter how hard I listened, you know, maybe it'd been too long, I didn't hear anything Isabelle thought anymore.

When we went back to the kitchen I held her hand again just so she could stand up on her high heels, Auntie Gina had prepared onion soup. Even when we had a feast at night, Uncle Jos always said man digs his grave with his teeth, I swear to God! We had to eat onion soup to fill holes and not risk a heart attack. We put bread in it. I went back to my usual seat, next to him, by the pile of *L'Huma des dimanches*, he had his back against the stove. Anita said goodbye to Auntie Gina, to Isabelle, she looked at her father-in-law who pretended not to notice. I didn't know what prison was. Some kids said it was when you looked too much at Renata's pussy and others that it was when we pinched Malabar bubble gum at Étoile des Alpes. I never had the courage to ask Uncle Jos. Maman was the only one who didn't make noise when she ate her soup. Edgar always left the onions on the side to eat only the crusty ends of the bread that float, then they sink to the bottom, good riddance.

The train was supposed to leave right at the time the news starts. Uncle Jos as I sometimes heard my ears say was a boor, especially when he couldn't watch the news in the middle of a historic period of change in the majority. Except it didn't change either in the end. I don't even want to tell you how Isabelle left, that shows you what a hard time I had downing the onions. At five till, Uncle Jos put on his Sunday beret, I went with Auntie Gina to the front steps. If I'm not president after boarding school when I'm eleven, maybe I could go to prison like my father. Maman hugged my head very tight and blocked my ears. She kissed me very quickly, I didn't have time to remember.

"Work hard, Edgar, be nice to Auntie Gina."

"Well yes."

"I'll call you. Talk to you soon."

"Well yes."

We would make each other's acquaintance.

"My name is Edgar, how are you?"

"Oh, hello Edgar. I'm doing well. And you, are you doing well too?"

"Well yes."

"You are my papa."

"Then in that case you are my son."

"Well yes."

"Would you like to have a Coke?"

Auntie Gina said goodbye, Madame Isabelle, come back soon to our beautiful village, have a good trip. She got in next to Uncle Jos. He had a garnet Citroën DS then that did a wheelie before taking off. I don't know what came over me, but as she was looking toward the steps where I was, I went to the window and put my hands on the glass so we could look at each other one more time, she said something to me aloud but I didn't hear, Uncle Jos slammed on the brakes. He would've smacked me if she hadn't been there. He was getting worked up under his beret and Isabelle looked at me, you know how, with you it's all open, like visiting an aquarium without moving, but with her it's all straight, right in the middle, where my name is Edgar I-don't-know-what. Auntie Gina rushed over with her Dago look and held me very tight in her arms. He started up again slowly toward the gate we repainted almost every year in the spring. Now Gina was holding my hand, hers didn't look at all like Isabelle's, I thought. She had done every type of work in the fields and she cut her neighbor's brambles. He'd been a pharmacist before ending up a cuckold by himself at home, with lots of empty bottles of wine on either side of the front steps that he no longer cleaned, and his orange gate that was a disgrace, for years, said Auntie Gina, years and years. Isabelle, hers were a little cold and very white, for putting on her rings and doing shorthand typing. Edgar felt the sadness of the century, she took me in her arms to see the DS drive away like a big toad on the bridge road, between the old rickety one next to the Paris–Geneva tracks and the Micheline that I never took. Gina sometimes had a tear in her eye, mind you, when Uncle Jos returned from meetings with too much white wine on his breath, or when Anita, who wasn't her daughter, came by to say hello to her all the same, but Uncle Jos didn't want her to come in, or even when Edgar wanted her to hold him in her arms.

"Stop it, Edgar, you look like the village idiot."

She was upset because if I'd been run over by Uncle Jos's DS she wouldn't have been able to keep the kids of unwed mothers, and that would've been the end of the road for her.

We closed the gate. Soon you wouldn't even have guessed the car had been by, but I still tried to hear Isabelle. I would've liked to go to the train station, but they hadn't wanted me to. I was of the age of reason, which is not yet the age to go to bed late. I don't know if it was the right train I saw. Since I'd been here, I'd never known if it was the one that came from behind the Sonzas, who were nice and very old and stone broke, they didn't have ten teeth between them, or the one that came backward. Auntie Gina would go to the Sonzas to buy eggs, the good ones made by Dago hens, and cheaper than at Étoile des Alpes. Then I went to bed.

The other kids who were more recent than me at Uncle Jos and Auntie Gina's were already asleep, except Renata. She had nightmares and ended up between Gina and Uncle Jos in his Damart thermals in the morning, or else when sometimes they made her leave she'd lie down by Carla's door, under a taped up picture of some degenerate English singers that they called Beatles. Carla locked herself in because she didn't want her room to be used as a shelter by Renata and the other kids, after her workday at the Social Security. Me, I slept. The next day, Uncle Jos was angry because he lost a Sunday and at night a road had broken into a thousand pieces. There had been a death. Sometimes the roads open up right down the middle, people fall in while waiting for help, or on the side of the road. That's what happened that night. We read the paper, he got the local news, Auntie Gina moved close to him and said, my goodness. He never read the obituaries which was the life of the dead, but shorter. Auntie Gina did it for him. Sometimes while he listened, he nodded as he poured himself some white wine, his blue eyes on the glass door, he asked the age of the dead person, and if it was too soon to end he got worked up about cold drafts. We'd never let death in as long as we were here, at Uncle Jos and Auntie Gina's, they could be confident of that. Besides, we boiled slugs, like I already told you, André and Annie helped their parents with the pig slaughter, the French sent Uncle Jos's party and the Bretons to get skinned at Stalingrad or Algeria, and in Mme. Nguyen's Vietnam. But above all what worried Uncle Jos most was falling rocks, car accidents, cigarette smoke, and especially heart attacks, that take you like a draft does, and you're already finished.

Sometimes it was Italians who filled the paper's obits page and he watched with eyes bluer than life behind the curtains. I know, he'd say to Auntie Gina, ah you see, stop, ah you see! When he said you see, it was bad, the kids would get a few smacks when he had nothing to add after his you sees, but he never dared with Auntie Gina. She always kept the big bread knife at her side, to make the Catholic cross on top and place it on the right side, against bad luck since the dawn of time, then he would have a fit. The kids were scared stiff in their chairs, Renata would start to bawl and find refuge under the table in the kitchen. Jean-Claude would go out without saying a word with his soccer ball like the one I got for my birthday, a big one that was black and white, heavy at the tip of the foot, when M. Vidonne signed me up for the U10-U11 team.

*

The rest before me, Madame Clarisse Georges, I'd like to try to tell you about, it was like that ball, heavy, and I wasn't used to it, I sometimes sat on it, like at the top of the field, where I'll often come back to remember, and other times I pushed it, all those years before, I liked them too. Gina held me in her arms, we went to the clinic. Edgar got a drop of blood pricked from the tip of his finger, apparently, she never talked about it, but Uncle Jos worried about blood cells, which are the army of living bodies until Stalingrad. I remember very little about it, except that it was also a good trip, to the clinic. Auntie Gina slipped on a black coat with a fur collar and we waited for the blue and white bus, she held her big black change-purse in her pocket and Edgar on the other side. While we waited for the bus we looked at the river, the dark and traumatized Fier, except when it froze, or if the snow falls a little, for a long time the water swallows it without a sound, the kids grab their boots and their hats and they go outside to play at fighting. Soon, our ears feel very warm. Auntie Gina smiles because she likes Dago games in the snow. Snowmen. She doesn't give us a carrot, so we don't waste food for nothing, but we take a stick from the wood-pile. We go back in, it's time for snack.

There it is, Madame Clarisse Georges, I spent several years like that, before me, I'm still in the Paris train and in the Dauphiné, Auntie Gina tells Uncle Jos about the dead. Often, they nab each other's glasses to read the paper, I'll have my own pair. In the winter, Gina, given that I'm the village idiot, lets me sit at the kitchen table after we eat. I look up words in the dictionary with her for her crosswords. Uncle Jos has already done the easy ones while drinking his coffee, she finishes them, the kids fart, sometimes we sing *Avanti popolo, bandiera rossaaaa!* We also listen to the radio when things happen. When he went to Paris for his party, Uncle Jos dressed like the leader of the French of Savoy, she looked at him with stern eyes and when he left, she made the sign of the cross on his forehead, ah see here, he answered. It was as if he was about to walk through the snow to go repair the roads, with all the kids surrounding Auntie Gina, he had an army on his side and shouldn't let people push him around. One of the road workers picked him up to take him to the train, often it was M. Rachex, of whom I have a very good memory because he died too, while I was there. Other times it was Letraz, but they weren't very friendly, he and Uncle Jos, because M. Letraz did as he pleased since he was French and especially since he could read, so Uncle Jos knew less about his life. In any case he hated Paris, where he went solely to prepare the revolution, because after boarding school as soon as I'm old enough to fight I'll return and then I'll be president. At first, I didn't get why Uncle Jos didn't want to be president himself because I was too little, you understand. His life was mostly about taking care of the roads so that people didn't fall in the holes, he would've never had time. There's a lot of roads. I still had double ear infections when I just got there, blood drops on the tips of my fingers, the dictionary, *La Vie ouvrière*, the end of the world is coming soon.

I see us leaving all together, the kids and Auntie Gina on the go-see road. She took the littlest ones by the hand, we all move forward in a line, nobody lags behind. We put two pairs of socks on, one on top of the other, and we lost our gloves. We were always late too, Mme. Lydie Vidonne, who didn't have kids of her own like Mme. Nguyen, waited for us at the school gate. Immediately, we put on our slippers. Edgar's had pompoms on top, I remember the pompoms well, Madame Clarisse Georges, anyway I don't have too many other things to remember. When it's nice out again we go to the soccer field.

Sometimes we take the bus that's called Ducruet and we goof around at the new stadium, Uncle Jos and the skeletons deputy had pestered some Dagos forever to get the field. M. Vidonne arrives in his 4L, puts on his shoes, I too had real soccer shoes, with cleats. My aunt from Ménilmontant had given them to me as a present. Her name is Aunt Meige, she often came to see me since I was paid for on a monthly basis. She arrived in a taxi at Auntie Gina and Uncle Jos's because she didn't like to bother people. She's from Ménilmontant.

In the summer, even longer ago, I saw glow-worms and also the fireworks on the 14th of July set off right over the river. The Dagos have the best fireworks, but they live like ragmen and Gypsies, still even Uncle Jos watched. Sometimes Auntie Gina went alone to visit her father, and when the kids went home on Saturdays, she would take me. He lived in a wood house that didn't always have electricity. He was very old and drank red wine and didn't want the light turned on. I can see well enough as it is, he always said to Gina. He smoked a lot of cigarettes like the worst of Uncle Jos's road workers, and he was very nice to Edgar your humble servant. He stank of tobacco, she cleaned his place grumbling *porca madonna* and he answered her:

"Gina, how are the children?"

He gave me wine to drink, *una gotta*, we fetched wood for him because he no longer wanted to move from the kitchen table where he was used to his memories, like Gina sometimes, after the meal with crosswords and the dead in the Dauphiné, sighed thinking of all of that. The kids were scared when she was like that. I was little at that time, but in the end, she'd always move forward, and bring us back up the go-see road, that's maybe called something else, but I got used to that name. Auntie Gina's father stayed in the dark all day long with his mustachioed old age in his village, I don't remember the name, smoking cigarettes without dying at all, except after Auntie Gina's eyes were all red, one evening.

It wasn't long after Isabelle had placed me with her on a monthly basis. Carla already had her 2CV that she called Titine or Dodoche to encourage it up the hills. Ordinarily, Gina let herself be driven with a fist on her heart, her daughter smoked in secret, and Auntie Gina sniffed around in the

Titine, it smells bad, you'll get in trouble with your father, *vavi ta more, vavi ta more*, which is a Dago phrase that scares people over there. The evening Gina got the phone call, Madame Clarisse Georges, Carla hadn't gone to make love in secret in town and that was good timing, she got dressed like for the Russian retreat, in a hurry. Carla had Uncle Jos's blue eyes. She wiped off her make-up before she got home.

"You know what that means," Gina said.

"Yes."

"You know what that means," repeated Auntie Gina.

"Yes, maman."

Edgar your humble servant heard everything, Uncle Jos was at a party meeting and Carla kept answering yes maman, Auntie Gina talked without saying anything at all in the car. Only Uncle Jos drove faster when he was drunk or when he left at night with the road workers to fill a hole. It was packed with Dagos in there, they'd only lit candles and Auntie Gina's papa's dog came to sniff me right away because no one wanted anything to do with him because of his fleas. Gina was crying without showing it because she was from the mountains. Dagos only cry when you go down toward the sea, where they're called Calabrian. Her daughter followed her with her eyes and they jabbered away in Italian, Carla had studied it at school. Auntie Gina went to wash glasses, get plates to put cakes in, I was sitting on a chair. Carla served and no one was talking anymore, some people made Auntie Gina sit down. They drank white wine, Edgar and the dog had some too. Then she went alone up to his room at the end of a wooden staircase like a ladder, in metal boxes on every step he kept his shotgun cartridges, his photos from the dawn of time that Gina loved, and the story of his life in shoeboxes.

I tried to hear what she was saying to him upstairs, but I don't remember. It lasted a while. I spent my first night since I was born sleeping on a chair. At some point, Uncle Jos arrived with his boots, before going upstairs he told Carla, who'd stayed there waiting for him, to take me home. He gave a kick in the butt to the dog whose name was Chamomile, like the tea you pick in September to dry it.

"All right, come on Edgar."

She climbed the ladder, maman, she said, papa is here, I'm taking Edgar home, I'll be back later. After that we left. First I also tried to give a kick to Chamomile, but since I was too much a kid, he went right next to my foot, yawning. I was sleepy, and Auntie Gina didn't have a papa anymore.

There were wet poppies in the fields, the fog rises above your boots in the morning. Auntie Gina's daughter smoked cigarettes that she held between three fingers, on the dash above the steering wheel, she had a little radio. You couldn't hear it well in the turns because of the squeals. The gate was closed, Carla told me, go open it for me Edgar, I went to push the black gate but since I wasn't all there I wasn't able to. I've always been afraid of the other side, Madame Clarisse Georges, even today, you know. Carla, when it came over her, yelled a little like Uncle Jos too. I didn't really want to come here when I was little, and then I didn't want to leave either. I would like to tell you about that too, why don't you have white wine if you like it, we got out of the 2CV and I went to bed.

*

Further back, I learned words, Auntie Gina had very beau- tiful handwriting, I had a hard time at first, she always said I looked like the village idiot, my tongue hung down onto the pages of the Rhodia notebook. Edgar, *a*, pull your tongue in, *e*, it's not a wet mop, *i*, I'm going to cut it off if you keep doing that, *o*, swallow it! We kept at it, and I managed. Uncle Jos arrived, he couldn't care less about consonants and vowels, he would say, come quick Edgar, presto! Let's go get the kindling. I was diligent. Starting when I was very small Gina made me copy letters too, I sent a bunch to Isabelle, I am very well, dear Maman, my ears are shrinking and my blood cells are going up, Auntie Gina is well, Uncle Jos is well, my teacher is well, the bone deputy is well, Nadino is well, Renata is well, the dog at Charmilles is not well but he's just a mongrel dog, so he's well too, and you? I hope you are well, and I knew how to sign Edgar without ever starting over. Auntie Gina bought cards from Unicef, which cares for the children of unwed mothers around the world, as indicated on the packet. She'd had so many kids in her life that she bought them in packs of 10, but we had to write a draft. I waited for Uncle Jos to come and send me to get kindling, little sticks to set fire to the already crumpled up *Humas des dimanches* and logs, so the fire would last. We sometimes went with him to cut them, all the kids in the woods, with the road workers who woke up when the sun did, said Auntie Gina, it was their job and it hadn't changed since the dawn of time.

I remember the trees that were about to fall, Uncle Jos has a drop on the tip of his nose that he wipes with the back of his hand, Godammit! Us kids run very far, the tree is already cut but it's still creaking, it crosses the sky in two parts. Uncle Jos just misses getting it on the head. When it's over he's in a good mood and we form a chain to put the logs in the wood-shed. With the kids, afterward, we sit on the stacks. The day I arrived, there were several cords, which are large packages of wood that you buy, next to the front steps. I remember it well because it was the first thing I did when I started to be paid for on a monthly basis over there, get the kindling to light the fire in the stove. The front entrance at Uncle Jos and Auntie Gina's had three steps, Isabelle had gone up first. I waited for her to come back and get me because I wasn't able to climb the stairs. My papa Bernard hadn't come because of his little family in Levallois-Perret. Maybe Isabelle would have worked up more courage with him but Gina knew very well how to talk to unwed mothers. Uncle Jos was messing with the logs and he said then, you're the new kid, you're as white as a Parisian turnip, I bellowed. Moooo, EdgAAr, EdgAAAr! He was less old than you at that time, his hair wasn't blond like a Savoyard's anymore but still a little yellow. He gave me some small logs, bring them to the kitchen. I bawled again because they were heavy. I went back to wait by the three steps at the front entrance, where Gina put flower pots with pansies in them, geraniums or sometimes chrysanthemums, she would make the rounds of the cemeteries. She cleaned the gravestones with bleach. I saw her take off her apron, the blue one with the white flowers. She rubbed her hands, she had a thin worn-out wedding band and she picked me up, me and the logs. I'm Auntie Gina, she told me, moo, EdgAAAr, EdGAAAr, I don't know how I remember that. The logs burned in the stove, we put the rest in a crate, and she said to me that's the stove, what can I say, Madame Isabelle, there's fresh air and a simple life in our mountains, Edgar pyromaniac.

The fire is blue at first when it's burning Sunday and then it becomes Monday, Madame Clarisse Georges, Edgar started filling the crate every day. At first I went with Uncle Jos or Auntie Gina and then after that I went alone with the other kids. We had the scare of the century if it was already dark and we'd forgotten to gather some for that evening. We took the flashlight that works with the big square Wonder batteries. That first time Isabelle had her very pensive look, you shouldn't worry too much, Uncle Jos was cheerful, what can you do, oh see here, he said to Auntie Gina, *vavi ta more vavi ta more*, I'd like to know what that means if you have an idea.

Then from the start of my being there, it was Auntie Gina who took care of Edgar, cotton in the ears and shit on the ass. On the train, Isabelle and I had fought a lot, but since we weren't in Asnières at home it didn't count. . . Auntie Gina who was the caregiver of a hundred kids, some of whom were already ten times as old as me, she got the medal they give for it, she wanted more. When I was a very recent kid my favorite song was by Richard Anthony, *I hear the train whistle,* blah, blah, blah, and right after that *avanti popolo, bandiera rossaaaa!* – the one about Edgar for president, we would go down to the Dutch river with our boots. Sometimes we'd catch sight of snakes and hornets, Uncle Jos also put bees to work in colonies around a big one called the queen, who can scarf down as much as she likes without doing any work. When he felt like it, he got stung on purpose by ten bees to get vaccinated, and then he didn't feel anything anymore. In 1965 Edgar would fall asleep with the train on the bridge departing from Gare de Lyon that must be coming to take me back, but no, blah, blah, blah, the train didn't whistle. It never whistled at all. In the cellar there was the big honey extractor, Uncle Jos turns the crank faster and faster and blood goes to his head, the kids go fetch the jars. He even gave some to Isabelle for when she went home to our place in Asnières. The following year, Aunt Meige came to buy some from him, don't even think about it, said Auntie Gina, because bees work for free, you only have to pay for the kid.

With my teacher Mme. Lydie Vidonne, we made crafts for Mother's Day, us kids from Auntie Gina's we had more work than the others because we made everything in twos, except

Renata who made three because of her older sister, who lived in Lyon in an emergency shelter after a stint turning tricks in a studio in Grenoble. The kids brought the jars, I liked all that, Madame Clarisse Georges, the honey flows and you can't move at all, because of the dust. We lick the plate under it. After that, I'm still quite a recent kid at Auntie Gina's, but I already know how to take care of the wild artichokes. You bury them in the cellar to blanch them and they make a fancy dinner treat, Edgar turns off the light, but I still prefer new potatoes, which are so small that the kids aren't allowed to scrub them because they lose half to the trash. I was going to go back there soon, I've grown up a lot you see. Maman left one evening, Gina had prepared a meal like for Christmases except instead of turkey she preferred a chicken from the Sonzas, Uncle Jos only killed slugs with the kids, or toads. She's the one who did the chickens. The kids had heard that before she was a waitress at a café. Uncle Jos had met her there. His blue eyes and hers very black and that was it, like never happened with Isabelle, even with my papa Bernard, who left shortly after me to join his family in Levallois-Perret. That's when I asked Auntie Gina about my own papa, the real one. So she took very good care of Edgar, she made me write cards, dear Maman, are you well, Auntie Gina is well, my ears are doing well, the bees are doing well, and you, I hope you are doing well, looking forward to reading a card from you soon because reading is going well too, and hello to all, your Edgar who loves you. Auntie Gina checked the Unicef card to make sure I had copied the draft correctly, she stuck the stamp herself with a quick lick of her tongue and wrote the address, Madame Isabelle in Asnières, past the General's Square near the cinema, under the bridge used by trains between Asnières and Bois-Colombes and Bécon-les-Bruyères then straight, Avenue de la Lauzière, near Caron Perfumes and the other row houses where the fences keep you from looking in, all the way to the third building on the square where we lived, Isabelle and I. Auntie Gina had gone to Paris on her honeymoon. When she wanted to have fun, she asked Uncle Jos to take her there, or else there'd be a Dago vendetta to pay. He raised his eyes from beneath his glasses if he was the one who had them and he muttered, oh see here, see here! He made a face like a mongrel dog or a kid faced with a plate of polenta or the liver steaks we had to ingest in little pieces at lunch time, and also on Fridays if Gina was angry.

When I left I was already half president of Savoy because I had been there the longest of the kids paid for on a monthly basis. After she decided for sure about boarding school, Isabelle stopped visiting me at Auntie Gina and Uncle Jos's, as if I were already back except I wasn't. I stayed for the summer and I knew a lot of kids and road workers. So Edgar, you're going to boarding school? You'll forget us. No I won't, I'd say to Uncle Jos. Gina gave him her stern Dago look and he looked at her unfazed. He didn't have children in the right majority, and he'd even had his seat at city hall stolen by Ricardo. Sometimes I went all by myself on the go-see road. Isabelle still paid the checks at the end of the month but I would return for the holidays for free. On the go-see road, André and his sister Annie caught grasshoppers, pulled off their legs, and scarfed them down like the Chinese do, I went with them. By now Carla had given me her whole bike because in addition to her 2CV she almost had a husband. Uncle Jos didn't smack her anymore now that she was engaged. She'd lugged her albums into town but she often came back to eat in the evening, or to spend part of an afternoon with Gina. I can't remember her husband who wore the firemen's uniform, he could climb a rope like an orangutan and dismantle a fireman's ladder all by himself. As for me, I would be leaving soon. Auntie Gina always went out of her way so we would have nice memories of her. Some kids wrote to her every year from further than Italy sometimes, because Dagos build houses everywhere they're needed, and some even do other things in life. Others didn't write to her. At times she was tired. For example, she would forget to turn the bread over on the right side and mark it with the cross, which meant a curse on your house, or else she would place both fists on her heart, and we kids waited to see if the world was ending and if it was a heart attack and what it might look like. She'd say ooh ooh, I feel dizzy, my head's spinning.

"Scram, off you go, shoo!"

We would go out onto the go-see road to piss in the watercress that always smelled like shit. From a distance looking back the house was small and the second one was even smaller in real life. Uncle Jos was having another one built when I left, in a place where there was no one. It was on a bare mountain with not even a mongrel dog running on the roads. I didn't know I would forget, on Edgar president of Savoy's word, we were all kids from Lyon, Saint-Étienne, Chalon-sur-Saône, and the Dago villages of Aosta and Torino, one time they took us to see the real land of Savoy in its entirety. Gina had exchanged French money for Dago money to buy things to drink and postcards to send to the unwed mothers. On the phone, Isabelle wouldn't tell me if she'd received them, only Auntie Gina, who asked her to find out if the mail was working. Yes, thank you, Auntie Gina. You're welcome, Madame Isabelle.

At night, while I waited for Uncle Jos to come up in his thermals making as much noise as an elephant on the stairs, I stayed at the window watching the train tracks, in case something happened. But what was boarding school? Edgar the noodle didn't have any idea, except it happens with priests who have seminaries to teach you how to give shit to Savoy, and in Ménilmontant, the beautiful church of Notre-Damede-la-Croix had a lot of steps to climb when I was little, before taking the train the first time. Finally, he arrived and had his evening coughing fit because of the smokers and the Jehovah's Witnesses who scared him before going to bed. I went to lie down. I couldn't go to sleep too well. You have to get an education, Uncle Jos repeated to me. Same as he knew about houses that held up, their foundations are more solid, and also, I'd have my own here when I came back. Auntie Gina didn't tell me that, I still wrote postcards to Isabelle and on Sundays, every other one I waited for her to call. She came with me into the room where Uncle Jos drew his plans.

"This is Maman, Edgar, are you doing well?"

"Well yes."

"And is school going well?"

"Well yes, it's over, we're on vacation."

"Hand me Auntie Gina."

"Well yes."

I immediately ran back to the courtyard to do a small chore. Uncle Jos always told the kids we don't feed you to do nothing, you have to work in life. He would start singing *bandiera rossaaa!* Auntie Gina made the sign of the cross for

the dead over whom no flag waves and she looked at us kids
and him. Nowadays she often went to the cemetery to put
flowers on her papa and other people, with trays of flowers
in containers she bought at the new Carrefour hypermarket
on the road to Geneva. Uncle Jos never went to the cemetery. At Carla's wedding, where Auntie Gina was the most
beautiful Dago with her black makeup on her eyes and her
very red lips, he took his daughter to the priest in a pearl-gray
suit with a white handkerchief in his breast pocket like a little
bird about to fly away, all the kids wearing short pants next
to Carla in her wedding gown. He walked so fast that it made
Ricardo and the others laugh, in case he started the revolution in the church and made a fine speech about the Battle of
Stalingrad. But he slowed down in time and behaved himself.

I was with Renata, and Anita, Ricardo's wife, who was nice
to the kids, took a picture of us all. It was part of my bag-
gage in 1971, when I found myself with my village idiot's
face and Isabelle waiting for me on the platform at Gare de
Lyon. Renata and Edgar were flower girl and page boy in
1971. I finally saw her pussy, it was for Edgar's last summer

at Uncle Jos and Auntie Gina's, we wanted to create memories just for the two of us. She was leaving for Lyon to join her older sister, but she would be back too. Renata always took up all the space in the skirts of the unwed mothers who came to visit their children, she needed to so badly, like the ones who met up with the cuckolds at Hôtel des Charmilles, except it's André who told me, I'd never seen anyone. In any case they say that the cuckolds of Charmilles make love and Mme. Nguyen sells them snake oils, Carla knew a lot of stories because she was the wife of a firefighter and worked at Social Security. She told them to Gina. Do you want to see my photo, Madame Clarisse Georges? Go ahead, see how I don't look like Edgar anymore, you'll have to admit I've changed, since I'm going to go back to Paris they cut my hair in a bowl cut. I don't even know if Isabelle will be able to recognize me. One day, Auntie Gina packed all my belongings. I can't remember why, but there wasn't much. I'd grown, I wore a lot of clothes that were handed down from the kids before me. Carla and her husband came, Ricardo and Anita too, we all had a drink. Us kids had Fruité, which is more expensive than mint syrup or grenadine. Edgar, in the photo, looks like the village idiot with his big ears. I had to go several times to the bathroom at the end of the hall to seem grown up, thankfully Uncle Jos and his son fought for a bit as usual.

Auntie Gina thought that unwed mothers already have too much to worry about in life, she said, be nice to your maman, she will be your maman, we would have to wash my whole body for my arrival at Gare de Lyon, when I take the train. We went to see my teacher the afternoon before. Auntie Gina held my hand to cross the road of the cuckold pharmacist who let brambles grow in our field, there was still never anyone there, she said hurry, Edgar, we're going to say goodbye to your teacher. Mme. Lydie Vidonne had gone to the beach for her vacation. I don't remember much, she mostly talked with Auntie Gina, Dago news, she was in the neutral zone as the kids' teacher and friend of Mme. Nguyen. M. Vidonne gave me a photo of the U10-U11 team, if you want to know about Jean-Claude and Nadino I'll bring it to you too, you'll see Edgar the noodle between the two of them, and we left.

"Well then, Edgar, see you soon, say hello to your maman for me."

"Well yes."

And I said hello to my maman for her.

I lived there for a very long time, because of my ears I could tell you as much as Uncle Jos about Stalingrad, the French, and the men who dig their graves with their teeth, there's something going on in my head where I'm not all there, now I know what it is. Mme. and M. Vidonne walked with us across the Jailbreak yard, where I didn't so much like to be prisoner. On the other side of the road, Mme. Nguyen has a flashing snake against the wall and also a cup because she makes potions. We had to buy bread at Étoile des Alpes, where it was under a new family. Mme. Nguyen came out at that moment, and in my opinion if you go out in the street and you see a short Chinese woman in a white lab coat you should ask her for me if she remembers Edgar, unless she's French I bet you it'll be her, Edgar, how are you? And how's your maman? Gina, how are you doing? We're all doing well, thank you, we went to the market. I looked at the cuckolds' cars to tell Renata about it who wanted to know if we knew other children like her in the region, she would soon be leaving for Lyon. Mme. Nguyen gave me some mints, thank you, Mme. Nguyen, goodbye little Edgar! She went back to preparing her magic potions, which she now sold all the way to the Swiss in Geneva, according to the deputy, who thought we'd become famous and Edgar president, especially since all the kids found skeletons full of bones for him.

We went home on the go-see road, I saw the Charmilles again. Nadino and André were kicking the dog to teach him a lesson. We went down the steps of the go-see road. I saw the mutt at that moment, he barked at me like he knew too. I can't say before I saw the dog that I'd really understood that I was leaving. I told Auntie Gina, but she didn't answer. No doubt she thought I was the village idiot but she held my hand very tight. When they're sad, Dagos talk very loud because they prefer to fight in life.

"You'll come back to visit us," repeated Gina.

"Well yes," I answered.

"Che sera."

The dog went off to lie in front of his bowl. Sometimes she said you'll forget us Edgar, she knew too many kids to be sure one hundred percent one way or the other, some come back and others don't. You have your maman Isabelle, come back and see us in our beautiful village, we're country folk. I wasn't strong enough yet to lift bales of hay with a pitchfork, now that I wasn't going to be paid for on a monthly basis anymore I wouldn't have to. Instead we went to the lake where Uncle Jos painted his rowboat, but with every layer he found that we hadn't used enough. The kids scraped the paint, once he'd called it Gina, in blue, but he changed his mind. In the end he put Stalingrad in red letters, so that all the people would know they should go take a hike. Auntie Gina always walked very fast, as soon as she left her house, she thought it would be the end if she wasn't there, she slowed down a little only before cleaning the gravestones. On the go-see road I felt really low, everything I'd seen that's where I'd seen it, maybe you understand a little, that this is the road I always drew in my notebooks, but I didn't want to rush. I want to come back, I swear, I said to Gina. That evening she made another meal of the century. Carla had stayed, her husband too, who was not from here but didn't mind having a house built for him.

Gina made me shine the shoes instead of putting the laces on them because it was an easier job, then I put my boots back on to go down to the field.

I had slow worms, which are tiny snakes that don't bite and I wasn't supposed to bring them to Gare de Lyon. The Fier had almost no water left at that time of year. The Findus frozen foods warehouse had been so fed up with freezing Dutch people after they drowned that they'd installed a tall barbed wire fence near the banks, but the kids could still go down through the brush at the bottom of Uncle Jos' field. We stayed, Edgar and the slow worms in the jar, everything was mixed up in my head, luckily Renata came to join me to show me her pussy, we played lovers again. Renata was full of stories in her head, she said to me, adieu, I am dying, Edgar my prince, then she died a little for real. And it would have been the end of everything if I hadn't started her up again by pulling on her panties, I brought her back to life.

"You have brought me back to life, Prince Edgar, let go of my panties. Hurry, we'll get in trouble."

Later, we went back up, we ate with everyone. I was next to Uncle Jos, he made a lot of noise with his spoon.

"So you're going away, you'll come back and see us."

"Well yes."

And he shrugged.

"What are you doing," mouthed Gina silently.

"Oh, see here."

Carla had brought a bottle of Asti, which is a very good Dago wine with bubbles that are almost pink. She poured a little for all the kids too. I still went back to the bathroom, and then when it was the new potatoes Edgar heard Gina, and we finished eating.

Everyone left, Uncle Jos put on his wool cap without saying a word to go watch TV. The kids cleared the table. Auntie Gina pulled out her Bic pen and her crosswords, I brought over the dictionary, and when we had prepared everything, I was able to cry really hard in her arms, your humble servant Edgar. Then I went to bed. I don't even want to tell you how much I liked the train, Madame Clarisse Georges, I had the seat by the window, because I had priority as the village idiot and future president too. I was almost eleven, Auntie Gina put my suitcase on the luggage rack, and that was it.

"Be nice to your maman, write to me."

"Well yes, Auntie Gina."

My Aunt Meige from Ménilmontant had come to get me because Isabelle couldn't, goodbye Madame, have a good trip, come back and see us, yes, of course.

"Edgar, wave to Auntie Gina."

She'd gone back down to the platform, I was already on the very comfortable train to Gare de Lyon. She was looking at the end of the platform with her stern gaze, Uncle Jos was waiting for her in the DS. The night before I'd heard him wheezing and coughing on the stairs and when he got to the top, I'd had to piss. We looked at each other in the hallway and he asked where're you going? To Paris, Uncle Jos, I answered. The two of us went to check for lights that had been left burning for no reason. I liked turning off the lights with Uncle Jos who blamed the electricity bills on them. Good, go to bed now. Aunt Meige was smiling at Auntie Gina, who was talking to us through the window, between the moment of the conductor's whistle and the train's departure there was a big silent hole, like on the suburban line that Isabelle and I took when I was just out of my consultations with you. I was waiting for something to happen, but Auntie Gina was looking at the opposite end of the platform with her dark eyes, at one point she smiled toward Edgar your humble servant and the train departed.

Then I waved like Aunt Meige who was looking outside and then at me, she had come to see me often all those years I spent over there. Auntie Gina started to walk with Edgar sitting above her on the seat, she was talking at the same time. But it must have been in Dago Italian I didn't understand despite my big ears, because I already couldn't hear anything anymore. She brought her face closer to the window where it was still *e pericoloso sporgersi* since 1964 and until now, cupping her two hands to make like a hallway for her eyes, which were black like the blue ones you have in my memory. Her lips were moving below, but I didn't hear anything because the vehicle had begun to pull out and Auntie Gina stopped following. Renata and Jean-Claude must have been in the garage shelling beans. I thought of them. I was the one who was supposed to come back, or maybe Uncle Jos would go to Paris again for a congress, although he barely had time to yell and he already wanted to come home to eat onion soup. When I stood up, the train left.

There we go, Aunt Meige said to me looking at her watch, right on time.

My Aunt Meige from Ménilmontant knew all the schedules by heart. If there was ever a delay, she always asked the conductors what was going on. I had to go to the bathroom. The train sped on through the hole in the toilet and I closed the lock, I made a big effort to piss, but I didn't have to go. I sat on it, Edgar president of French Savoy, with a bit of Dago. Aunt Meige was waiting for me and at one point when the hole was moving so fast that I couldn't count the rails she came knocking on the door.

"Edgar, are you all right, are you almost done?"

"Well yes."

We returned to our compartment.

"Good, let's eat some cookies, would you like that?"

Aunt Meige brought out chocolate cookies, she chose the

best ones, we scarfed them down, and I got some on purpose on the pants that Auntie Gina had ironed for me for Gare de Lyon.

I went back to the toilet to wipe myself off, Aunt Meige gave me a handkerchief. The trip started to last a long time. We went over the bridge in the direction I thought and I yelled like a real moron from Rue d'Avron, look Aunt Meige, it's there, it's there! She said, yes, it's there Edgar, with her kind smile, there were only six of us in the compartment. We read *Le Dauphiné* that she had bought at the train station but not *L'Huma des dimanches* nor *Réveillez-vous* which were really my favorite newspapers, because of the stories, the fire that crumples them and time goes by, Edgar is getting older. Aunt Meige also had candy in her handbag, we did the crosswords. She went very fast, she was so used to trains, she worked at the train station at Gare de L'Est, and I have to arrive soon on the platform at Gare de Lyon, which is the end of it all for Edgar your humble servant.

*

Maman had the same gaze as I remembered from before. We waited for the complete stop of the vehicle. I wasn't able to take down the suitcase by myself. We're here, said Aunt Meige. She looked at her little gold watch with the clasp on it, right on time. She liked trains that were always on time, I did too. We ended up in the corridor with the other travelers. I think I'll leave you alone for a while, Madame Clarisse Georges. Maman had walked up the platform, she saw Edgar first, I had something like a cardiac attack between my temples, her head reached to *e pericoloso sporgersi*. She wore her hair in a bun now, like Auntie Gina sometimes did for celebrations or Christmases and funerals.

"Ah, there's your maman."

"Well yes."

Isabelle was smiling only on the bottom where her lips didn't move, she still had the same gaze in 1971 as in 1964 and at Parc Monceau, and at night when we went to bed.

My name is Edgar, I'm not all there, and I'm going to boarding school. There were two steps to exit the train car. Be careful, said Aunt Meige, they're not both the same height, Edgar. Aunt Meige was going to go back to Ménilmontant.

This is where we get off, Madame Clarisse Georges, I don't know yet if I'm going to go see you right away or else later, remember my name, Aunt Meige gave me a hug and said see you soon, she had to go to work. She went to mail the card I wrote to Auntie Gina and Uncle Jos on the train after the crosswords, but this time I hadn't done a draft. What should I say? I asked Aunt Meige, the trip went well, we're arriving soon at Gare de Lyon, my maman is there, here all is well, and you? Edgar is well.

There it is, the little fatty with the dandruff in her hair you can let her in, and then after that go on holiday at Hôtel des Charmilles, but watch out for the dog, make sure he leaves you in one piece. Tell them Edgar president sent you, tell them I'm well, and them, are they well? After that you'll return refreshed, you'll wipe your glasses and it'll be Edgar next.

THE FIRST
BOARDING SCHOOL

I SAW THE SEINE again in 1971, when I went home. There were still barges moored at the quay, an emptied swimming pool right at the edge, on the riverbank in Clichy, near the big cemetery. It was there. We barely said hello she and I, we didn't have much time. On the other hand, it was all new in my room. Maman must have done a lot of shorthand typing in my absence, she'd changed all my things. Of the building where I lived before, I still recognized the entrance, the mailboxes and also the walls painted yellow in the stairwell. I had a big bed now, wallpaper with toy soldiers because I was little man Edgar, a storm lamp like on the deck of a boat on the wall above my bed. Isabelle, at first it was her hairdo that surprised me on the platform at Gare de Lyon. Then, we just

147

looked at each other sideways, she and I, as if we'd already forgotten what to say to each other, and on the bridge to the trains I understood that my trip had ended.

Around Asnières where we lived it hadn't changed much, even if I didn't remember well, except when I told the kids about it at Uncle Jos and Auntie Gina's. The Seine flowed, always in the same direction, and then after the Clichy-Levallois station, you could see the Sacré-Coeur church well if you turned your head. Sometimes, in my new room, I did like Auntie Gina a little sign of the cross on my forehead to cast away misfortune, which is about all Edgar can look forward to at boarding school. I understood about boarding school. I'd looked up the word *intern* in the dictionary. It was right in the middle, between the *interzone* where peaceful gods live and the *Internationale* that Uncle Jos sang at congresses. Boarding schools were used to keep kids until they were grown up. I loved the dictionary.

Isabelle walked fast on the platform in the métro and at the train station. Her gaze came back to me from far away, always the same too, as if she were looking at someone in her head

148

and not at me. And I didn't know who it was. I had a hard time understanding. We went through Gare Saint-Lazare on the side with the lockers, which are metal boxes where you can hide things and keep the key, and not worry about where you're going next – you could always go back. She also had a new handbag that was midnight blue. And then the Seine passed beneath us again, like a big snake that crosses the whole world, and all kids ask themselves one day or another where it goes and what will happen when they encounter it, I said oh, the Seine! to Isabelle, but I didn't bellow so I wouldn't hurt her feelings. I didn't want her to think I was still the same moron from Rue d'Avron. She looked straight at me with surprise, as if there was no doubt now that I was there. There were two Edgars in the dictionary, but there were four Édouards next to them, with their portraits so you wouldn't mix them up. Maybe there would be three when I was the president. Meanwhile, Maman sighed to give herself courage, Edgar the noodle was coming home.

I don't remember how many days we stayed together before I left again. Not many anyway. The first night after a long train ride you still feel the beat in your legs, even without having walked or run. As soon as I arrived, Maman had me take a shower in the half-tub. She picked up all my clothes to take them to the Lavomatic laundromat near the square. After that we ate while listening to the radio.

"Go to bed, Edgar."

Isabelle turned her cheekbone toward me.

Just like before when I wasn't all there, she always took off her rings to make meals or at the sink, now she had a new one, dark blue. I'd already seen it the last time and wondered who it was from. After that she made a phone call, but I didn't feel like listening. In 1971, in the evenings when I wasn't at boarding school, it was telephone time. Isabelle waited until Edgar left her alone to make a call. Now she spoke even less than before, when I was little, except sometimes in the kitchen her lips would move, without a sound. We'd look at each other from time to time, and then she'd tell me to go to my room. Sometimes she peeked in at the door to see if I was having a good time.

After I'd gone away again, we went to the department stores near Gare Saint-Lazare. Isabelle wasn't doing shorthand typing, she'd taken a few days off without leaving – because that's what unwed mothers prefer I think, stores where they take the escalator to look at the things they can't buy, and nobody says anything to them. Sometimes Aunt Meige met us at the War Memorial at Gare Saint-Lazare, where the names of the people are lined up with their ages, there are flower wreaths at the foot. Aunt Meige rushed around a lot too, even Edgar on the bike on the go-see road never went as fast as they did on their way to the department stores. I liked the Galeries Lafayette, mostly because of all the people you saw there. Isabelle looked surprised when I wanted to talk to her about before, as though it had never existed. When she didn't answer, I quickly dropped it.

One evening on the phone she said to someone that I was getting used to it, yes yes, he's going to boarding school soon, when will you be back? Her voice wasn't like it had been before either, since I was going to become president of Savoy I was on scholarship for my studies in the meantime. Aunt Meige bought new clothes for me at Printemps. Printemps is another very large, fancy department store where you see unwed mothers on every floor with their kids. They do back-to-school shopping. Afterward the unwed mothers go back to shorthand typing, dreaming of the things they saw, while their kids end up at boarding school, which is the place you park school children. I especially remember the escalators, you pass the people going down who you may never meet again, that was one of the things Edgar liked. With Aunt Meige, we sometimes went to eat cakes at the top, under the cupola, sometimes she took my hand on the escalator and sang, as if it were Ménilmontant forever in life. But I don't think it's true. With Isabelle, we often stopped on the ground floor, where there are all the perfumes in the world and free samples.

I remember that with Maman we also had time before boarding school to visit family, it's Edgar he's back, hello Edgar, are you well, Edgar?

"Well yes."

Their breath had the same smell as I remembered, and they also had a funny accent, is Uncle Jos well? Is Auntie Gina well? Isabelle didn't like her maman, who always made stuffed tomatoes for us, is it good?

"Well yes."

Here in Ménilmontant, it was still the same except for belote, no one played it anymore like when I was little. Isabelle's maman lived near the grand Boulevard de Ménilmontant, on a little street where no Dagos lived but there were Arabs, people said they fought with knives at night. I thought they had beautiful black eyes as if they were looking for water in the desert. They reminded me of the Gypsies from the little circus with the donkey Cadichon, who traveled from village to village where they made kids laugh under their tent. They returned every year. They kept their knives to themselves. We walked very fast on Boulevard de Ménilmontant, watching out for all the things that might happen to us.

"Finally, here you are," said Isabelle's maman.

"That's right, who else could it be?"

They didn't hug either, like Isabelle now did with the Edgar package, they turned their cheekbones to each other. When it was my turn, Maman immediately took out a handkerchief to wipe off the red lipstick. Unwed mothers wore it every day around here, but right after putting it on they pressed their lips together and even with my super ears in 1971, I couldn't hear anymore.

That year if you wanted to see Edgar on Saturdays when he wasn't at boarding school you'd wait until two o'clock in the afternoon, then you'd see a lady with bright blue eyes and a small Clic-Clac umbrella, her gaze turned to the names of the dead on the memorial. Edgar would be right in front of them and he'd fart in their faces, it'd be Aunt Meige who's there. My Aunt Meige didn't have children. She worked in trains, she liked trips and cookies. With my big ears from before, I'd heard she'd met a Dago as rich as Uncle Jos's party, he'd told her *ti amo*, but she'd answered him, me not *ti amo*, so *ciao*, and she took good care of Edgar. One day, when I'm the president, I'll appoint her to take kids by train to Auntie Gina's, on arrival and departure they'll scarf down lots of cookies to give themselves courage. Around six she took me back to Gare Saint-Lazare, we'd had a nice day. Now under her eyes that she made up, Isabelle had words that she said to herself, she took pills that she dropped in a half glass of water, she was feeling so bad. Before, us kids would always fill them to the brim, now it wasn't allowed. Otherwise, it's the end of everything, if they keep at it kids start to resemble their fathers and they end up you know where. I was supposed to stay in my room.

I had a desk with two drawers, often Edgar the noodle is sitting on his chair. There are no crossword puzzles to do here, there's no *L'Huma des dimanches* crumpled in the fire and there's no *Réveillez-vous* either, there's no playing outside. I have to close the door to my room. Edgar yawns at home, his maman is in the kitchen, she closes her lips and crushes words, she smokes Craven A. Uncle Jos would have a fit if he saw her. In the evening, after the telephone, she sews my name in my underwear, my undershirts, all my clothes, and then one day that's it, we take a new train, which is Edgar's train to boarding school. Aunt Meige had bought me a satchel with straps like to go on a trip and Isabelle a big red bag to put my things in. It was a very long way. You had to switch in Enghien, Isabelle read a magazine. Afterward she had to return to work in a new place. She was in a hurry to drop me where I was going, with my name on the clothes so there would be no mistake. To go to boarding school, you switch trains, two stations, then you take a bus. Isabelle asks which one it is, people hesitate, she sighs. And then I thought for the first time in my life, since the trip was so long, does Isabelle love Edgar, is she my maman, and who is my papa? But I pretended like I'd put on lipstick too, I didn't ask her right away.

*

When we arrived in front of the boarding school, I saw a large black gate and some trees. Further away, on the path behind a pond, priests without black cassocks but with suits like Uncle Jos for congresses and a little cross on the lapels of the jackets waited for the kids. They all had the same smile, as if they too had gone to a school to learn. Maman and I nonetheless stopped at the gate for a bit, she looked at me funny, and then off we went, come on Edgar, let's go.

"Well yes."

As I walked, the sound of the train stopped completely on the way to the building, as if I would never again be four, six, eight, or ten years old, I had to go to the bathroom.

"I have to pee, Mama. Where is it?"

All the unwed mothers were arriving in a hurry it'd been such a long journey, some kids came with their two parents too.

"Hold it in, Edgar, just a minute."

"Well yes."

We went in the big building and all sat down, then we all had to stand up one by one and when it was my turn, I could tell because Maman looked at me, like when I was called in at Rue d'Avron. I stood up, hello Edgar, hello, I answered. When they finished roll call we lined up, which is something I knew how to do from Uncle Jos and Auntie Gina and the U10-U11 soccer team. We had to go upstairs to the dormitories, which were full of metal beds, with the names sewn on the blankets Isabelle had already sent. We all made the beds with the unwed mothers and the real or fake fathers, I wasn't sure, you can't tell the difference right away. We were two kids per closet.

At first it was as if Isabelle was taking my place at boarding school, and I was the one who would go take the train back to Gare de Lyon, but actually the bed was too small, so at the last minute all the kids stay on purpose, and it's the unwed mothers who leave with their shorthand typing to do. Father Duluc has his hands behind his back and the Edgar package is twisting because he has to piss and shit so bad. He feels like asking him if he knows Uncle Jos because Uncle Jos had wanted to be a priest for a bit when he was young, but then he'd chosen Stalingrad, that's why screw them. Father Duluc was older than him, he was even older than all the dead from the memorial at Gare Saint-Lazare lined up end to end. When I imagine him he stays with his little smile, his hands clasped behind his back, all the priests at boarding school do that. Their hands are white like they're shorthand typists when in fact their work is just to watch the kids and pray for all kinds of things at once, diseases, wars, parents, studies, thanks, forgiveness, the Virgin Mary, who is an immaculate unwed mother, her son who was nailed to the cross, and the end of the world. I thought at first they forgot to pray also for the end of the world, but they kept the best for the end. Name, says Father Duluc, Edgaarrr, good, go to the court-yard, Edgar.

Isabelle after the bed left to see the head of the others. He was called Father as if it was the unwed mothers who'd chosen him and paid for him on a monthly basis too, and I open my ears wide, the chestnut trees in the courtyard are very tall, the kids start kicking the burrs. So another one that we were supposed to call Brother so we didn't mix him up takes out a whistle, the kids stop, he takes out a small black notebook, name, he says, Edgar, I answer, and I still had to piss just as much at that moment. Isabelle had put away my things in the closet I would be sharing with another kid. His name was Victor, his nose was crooked, his eyes were blue and his hair curly, I had the big droopy ears and short hair.

"I need to go pee, please, Father, you mean urinate, Father Monluc says to me, well yes, is it urgent, name? Edgar. . . Edgaarrr. Maman hadn't dared to ask for me. So he wrote my name in his notebook and he said Edgar, I'm watching you.

"Well yes," I answered.

He pulled his hand from behind his back to show me the stairs of the building, which we call the château, the boarders live in the château, or more like a large structure, as you can see ladies we have a magnificent setting, but all the same that does not mean that we live like royalty here. All the unwed mothers smiled and as a result their kids all had the runs at the same time, we left one after the other to the toilet. There was another one at the door, name, Edgaarrr, Father, I'm watching you, well yes, but I didn't say anything else this time. I only thought that I didn't feel like being here at all, and I stayed in the bathroom for a long time, you know Edgar.

The meeting was over when I came out, I went back to the courtyard. At one point we took out balls to show the unwed mothers our recess activities, we formed teams. Before I was in the U10-U11, I said, I was on M. Vidonne's team. Is that so, who is M. Vidonne?. . . . Since it would have taken a long time to explain I didn't answer, but the Father didn't write me up this time. I sat on a bench with the kids who didn't feel like playing, at one point Isabelle came out of the Fathers' office. Father Monluc, who was watching us, immediately walked toward her with his hands behind his back, he was shorter than Isabelle, they came toward Edgar together, chatting. Now Maman was smiling, despite her dark and trauma-tized gaze, seeing how she could be confident, because I was once again being paid for on a monthly basis, with also the little black notebooks to know everything from a distance, how practical. In the evening, I wrote a card to Auntie Gina, Edgar is well, I've started boarding school, all's well, and you Auntie Gina, tell me, I send you a hug, and then I put the card in my school bag with the straps. I planned to give it to Aunt Meige. I never sent the card. I don't remember how long Isabelle stayed. When the unwed mothers started to leave, she turned her cheek toward me, as though she had just seen me, before here, before me, and I was just passing through, good luck, see you soon, Edgar, work hard.

"Well yes."

I saw Maman walk back toward the gate, she soon turned around, I couldn't see her eyes from here, instead she raised her hand, which means goodbye and see you soon. It was always the same since I'd been born at Rue d'Avron. After Maman left I wanted to return to the bathroom to think for a minute about what was happening to Edgar, but we didn't have time. Instead we had to line up to listen to the Father of Fathers, who's called the Sup, all the kids in front and the priests on the stage, nuns too, like I'd never seen before, with headdresses in their hair, English women I'd never met in Parc Monceau, without handbags to store their keys and the photos of their kids at boarding school somewhere, but instead with their arms folded behind their backs and little notebooks in their pockets. Edgar, I said to myself, I can't remember what, we were in the lower school. It's as if I was starting everything all over again, I didn't really understand why, I don't even remember what I said to myself, on Edgar's word. I had the scare of the century, and I was no longer allowed to go to the bathroom because of the next meeting. We sat down to start learning about life, but then we had to get up again because we had to sit down all at the same time, as if we had just one ass divided by two butt cheeks into fifty kids equals one hundred. I thought very hard of Auntie Gina so she would come, and poof, there she was. She said, Edgar, you look like the village idiot, well yes, I know, you always say the same thing, Auntie Gina. Sit down correctly when Father Monluc says to! But he speaks very quietly, I said to Auntie Gina, it's on purpose she answered, it's to have silence in the ranks. *Vavi ta more vavi ta more*. The kids from the lower school sat back down, fifty times two butt cheeks equals one hundred, is this good Father? he asked the Sup. Yes, that'll do for a start. My caregiver took advantage of that moment to do the little Dago sign of the cross on my forehead, *vavi ta more vavi ta more,* then she put her hand over Uncle Jos's mouth who'd just arrived in his Damart thermals and wanted to sing *avanti popolo* to show them who Edgar was. They quickly dissolved again into being not all there, like at the end of a movie. Uncle Jos was yelling behind Auntie Gina's hand, and I stopped forever being three, four, five, six, seven, eight, nine, and ten years old at that moment, and I couldn't hear anything anymore. I never heard anything again.

*

After roll call, the Sup continued his speech. Some of our parents had made sacrifices so we could be lucky enough to be here, they're called scholarship pupils. Victor, who was from the same closet as me, and I, we looked at each other, then at a big kid who was being made to stand up by himself because he'd arrived late, he even had a Dago name, Londerio, the only Dago name I'd noticed up to now. Father

Monluc no doubt wanted to write his ass up in his notebook so he'd have us all down, repeat, he said, the big kid stuttered, Fabrizio lon lon Londeriiiiooo! And you? Edgaar, Edgaaarr! Where'd you get that accent? From Uncle Jos and Auntie Gina, no talking in the ranks, Edgar, understood?

"Well yes," I answered.

"And you?"

Victor from the same closet stood up very fast, my name is Victor Segalen, then he sat back down with his hands behind his back. He told him in a whisper to go fuck himself, I'd never heard that word, which wasn't in the dictionary. He was smiling at Father Monluc. Then it was the other kids' turn. We toured the premises in single file, the classrooms were all prefab, then the château, the common room, the dormitory, the showers, the chapel, that was for praying, because it was the house of the Father, we were told. Edgar, with what was not all there, didn't have enough room for all that. It was quickly decided.

I think I wanted to go back home right away, to make sure I opened my ears wide some more, I tried to listen very far over by the train bridge, I even tried to listen in on Isabelle.

She'd just turned around by the gate and we looked at each other, her whole gaze in mine. I'd said to Father Monluc, who was watching the direction of the traffic, don't sweat it I'll be back. And the extraordinary thing that Edgar the boarder in 1971 would like to tell you is that Isabelle turned around, and since I had my ears turned all the way up, she understood. All of a sudden Maman untied her hair and started running toward me in her shorthand typist's high heels, in fact Father Monluc took out his little black notebook like Auntie Gina had for her figures, but Father Duluc stopped him, no Father. She's in the unwed mothers' line, she's not from the lower school, ah yes, you're right, I should really wear glasses. But already I couldn't hear them any longer, Isabelle and I were in each other's arms now, and she said to me, good, quickly, let's go home.

"Really?"

"Yes, sweetie."

Which goes to show 1971 was a good year too, you see. We took the bus back to Enghien, there was a lake on the way and a casino for gamblers who'd lose a fortune in colorful chips and go off on boat tour where there were a miraculous amount of fish. My papa, if I'm to believe my big ears, Madame Clarisse Georges, was a bit of a casino gambler. He must have spent his life on the lake, since his pockets were always full of chips.

"That's bullshit, Victor said to me after lights out. That's not possible. That's not true."

Victor was taller than me, Fabrizio's feet totally stuck out of the bed in the dormitory, me, I was normal sized. Victor slept with a handkerchief in his hand, at first I didn't understand why. After lights out the Fathers went to their own house and the dorm monitors with flashlights took over. Edgar ever since the boiler wasn't afraid of the dark anymore. M. Lassale was in charge of the lower school, at first he was nice, we could be informal with him if we wanted. He made his rounds at ten, after the rounds Victor showed me what his handkerchief was for. The first nights I heard all kinds of strange noises but there weren't any animals like where I was before, my ears nearly fell off, on Edgar's word. I remembered the Clauds' field. I immediately decided not to do like Victor more than once a day because at eleven it makes you deaf, a few weeks later blind, and I might be dead before I even got to be president. M. Lassale wore slippers called Charentaises so he wouldn't make any noise, but with my ears there was no risk, you understand.

In the morning we get up, the entire lower school goes to brush their teeth, and Father Duluc arrives. We go down to the dining hall, where we have a bowl with a plate on top. First we say thanks for the meal, then we go get coffee with milk. Father Duluc settles in on the stage, and it's fifty times two butt cheeks equals one hundred, it's not such a pleasant memory, I have to say. Then we go to class in the prefab. The monitor plays guitar, on the way we could ask him things. Fabrizio Londerio had big shoes, his feet walked inward, he was always behind. Sometimes the entire lower school had to stop and wait for him. Fabrizio didn't even have an unwed mother, whereas Victor had his in Enghien, a father in another place. Edgar too I told myself, he must have one somewhere, I invented a lot of them for myself that decade. Mine went fishing and also took journeys. Victor's father was in La Santé prison, or he'd change his mind, and he was a soccer player because the Sup had given permission for us to watch matches on TV. Edgar has droopy ears and a funny accent. He doesn't know what fucked means and he doesn't learn his lessons well. He isn't all there, for sure. The day pupils arrived at eight. We often fought.

It's strange, I remember the boarding school very well, Madame Clarisse, but it's not the same color as before. I've grown up. At night, the youngest ones in the lower school sleep and make unwed mothers for themselves out of pillows. Sometimes Edgar tries to cover his ears and go back to Gare de Lyon. When I was eleven I still heard pretty well, when I covered my ears. But I heard less than before, you know. I could hear: Man digs his grave with his teeth, there are cracks in the road to Meythet, *vavi ta more*, Uncle Jos's rowboat on the lake has changed color again. I hear the words Isabelle crushes with her lips. With those I tell myself stories, I make up the one she doesn't tell me. The Sup is a little bald guy, who has a lot of things to do, when he passes through the dining hall, or the classroom, we stand. I was still a quiet, unassuming child, you see. I made up what I didn't know. I didn't know much.

"Where's your father?"

I'd have liked to know that myself. Victor wasn't a very good friend, what he liked most was fighting. His mother called him on the phone, Isabelle also called me in the beginning.

"It's Maman. Are you well Edgar? And classes? Don't forget to wait for us at the bus Saturday."

"Well yes."

Edgar cries one night and the monitor notices. He turns on his flashlight and he sees the village idiot, his ears limp on the sheets. He comes around to make sure we put our hands on top not beneath. He was from Brittany, he told us over and over, he drove to Paris in a Citroën 2CV.

"Why are you crying Edgar?"

"For no reason."

"Do you want to talk about it?"

I opened my ears wide. But I wanted to talk, Madame Clarisse Georges.

"Well yes."

We go to his room, sit down. You're not happy here?

"Well no."

So I tell him about the Battle of Stalingrad, about Auntie

Gina and Uncle Jos, Isabelle and shorthand typing, he listens to me while smoking a cigarette and says to me:

"All right, go to bed now, you're going home soon."

The days get shorter and go faster into night. On Thursdays, the boarders are blessed in the chapel by a miracle of God and they thank their parents for their sacrifices. When we leave the château, Fabrizio because he's slow is always last in line, the kids say he's a moron. He doesn't know the name of the place he comes from anymore. He has no parents at all. He's traveled a lot too. The tables are too small for him, so he's kept aside, in class he has one all to himself where he can stretch his legs with his pigeon-toed feet. Isabelle doesn't call me anymore, I'm already used to it. In class, it's going well, my grades are going well, but Victor says I'm a faggot, I'm the little Parisian who belongs to no one at boarding school. I have dreams at night. The monitor keeps changing the batteries in his flashlight. I don't like Lassale, he told the Sup everything. Maybe that's why Isabelle chews up her words? Because she doesn't want to tell? I want to know. The Sup walks into Classroom 3 near the crematorium for things from the dining hall, behind the prefab. That's where we take a shit when we really have to go. Sometimes we set fire to stuff that's lying around. Now I prefer to hang around with Fabrizio, he's still pigeon-toed but I have my ears and also my nose now. Victor says I have a nose like a yid. Yid is the word above Yurt, a Mongolian tent. Edgar's growth spurts started with his face. Victor likes to fight. Fabrizio is from Piedmont, he knows Dagos. Victor is afraid of him. Also, Fabrizio doesn't know why they moved him, he struggles to remember his lessons and he speaks French badly. *Vavi ta more*, I say to him. That makes him laugh.

I, Edgar president, am the boarders' first dictionary. When I use the one in the common room, I look in the back after the pink pages with the citations, for the names Uncle Jos used to tell me, Stalingrad, Stalin, and I also think about Aunt Meige, she says she's going to take me to the movies soon. Victor isn't a good friend, Fabrizio doesn't tell him anything. He doesn't talk to him, and if he messes with me he hits him. But he's afraid in French class, with M. Ziniac the sadist. Sadist comes after Sacrum, one of the bones the deputy had us dig up from where I was before, also Sacrosanct, which is for the houses of the Father in France and maybe even where the Dagos are, your humble servant Edgar. Me, it's old sister Mary from the British Empire who scares me. She has the same glasses as you, Madame Clarisse Georges. Saturday afternoons the boarders in the lower school leave to be with their unwed mothers. Fabrizio, who is a head taller than us, stays in detention because he doesn't know French well and has no one to go to. Victor isn't on the bus with me, he goes in the Fathers' blue van and takes the train to Enghien. I have my red bag, we're in a year where the red bag is the main thing, often I'm afraid to go home because when I forget things, Isabelle gets angry. Since I'm not all there, I forget my underwear, my socks, my notebooks. So Maman started checking me again like before. I go see Aunt Meige, so Edgar, are you doing well? And we go to the movies. It's an animated film, you don't need much to be happy. The bear sings, Mowgli has to go back to his home because he isn't little anymore. The snake has eyes that spin. The old panther walks silently, and then Aunt Meige takes me back to the train at Gare Saint-Lazare. The Rex is the biggest movie theater of the Boulevards. I had to tell Fabrizio about it again and again.

I never liked Sundays, Madame Clarisse Georges, when it was morning Isabelle stayed in the kitchen, taking her little pink pills, and she was angry because of Edgar, often I didn't know why. I was still just the Edgar package, I said to myself, that must be why. So I made as little noise as possible in my room.

One day when the bus arrived Edgar already had the runs from having not wiped well during the week at boarding school and I had another surprise of the century, he was very tall too. He was smoking a cigarette, his brown hair combed all the way back, very blue eyes. He was looking straight ahead when I arrived, looking farther away than Edgar. It was the first time since my return to Paris that I was carted around in a car, but it's strange, I don't remember the make. His name was Jean-Pierre. That's when I learned that Isabelle wasn't a shorthand typist in the glass building anymore. She was a secretary in Paris, still with a very long commute. Jean-Pierre turned his cheekbone toward me, then we went home. When he got in his car he looked at me in the rearview mirror, I'd never seen a man like that before. When we arrived home,

Isabelle immediately took all my things out of the red bag, the weather outside was very bad, the rain pounded against the window of my room. Jean-Pierre was looking at me. I was missing a pair of underwear and a sock, Isabelle sighed like never before. Edgar was a great worry to her in 1971.

"That's a bit much, Edgar. Go to your room."

Then she calls me and we eat. At dinner Maman still has a dark and traumatized gaze but now there's a bottle of wine on the table. She calls him JP, he calls her Isa, I don't understand everything when he talks to her. I listen carefully though. Jean-Pierre talks about his life, his work, his family, his own childhood, he thinks there's some good to corporal punishment. Isabelle nods, yes, yes, he's going through a rough patch at work, but he'll recover. He's a sales manager. His own father was strict, that's why he's done so well in life.

I go do my homework in my room, I take out my things. I'm sitting at my desk and look out the window. I'd like to go back out. We'd go for a walk alone, Isabelle and I, like maybe we used to do before. Earlier on the bus and again in JP's car I saw the Seine, I'd like to go for a walk there, maybe it's changed after all, I see it every week. Yes, she's changed for sure if you look at her closely. Auntie Gina still writes to me, when I return from boarding school Isabelle has already opened the card and she tells me, go to your room, Edgar the noodle, what should I say, thank you for your card Auntie Gina, school is going well, my maman is well, hope to see you soon. Your Edgar. Soon is far. I can't count all the way to soon. I don't like that word. I'll be president when I grow up.

We sometimes went to Ménilmontant, Isabelle dressed even better than before. Jean-Pierre often traveled for work. In the evening, they take Edgar back to the bus. First Maman puts my red bag on the table and Edgar must sit in front of it, two shirts, three pairs of socks, plus the one he forgot makes four, she takes her pills, go to your room immediately. I tell myself she's blown a fuse, I'll fix that when I grow up. She also gives me cheese for when we get there in the evening. At the dining hall on Sundays not everyone is there yet; there're asses missing to make a hundred, some boarders won't arrive until Monday morning. So we're allowed to sit without waiting for the bell. I'm happy to see Fabrizio again, now he wants us to call him Fabrice so it sounds less Dago. But that doesn't straighten his pigeon-toed feet. On Sunday nights he waits for me by the gate. Then it's the end of the night.

He stutters when M. Ziniac comes into the class, with his little mustache and his crew cut. The sadist smokes cigarillos that he crushes with the heel of his shiny black shoes, and we have to stand with our hands behind our backs. He enters the prefab and slams the door. Edgar is in the third row, Londerio, stand up! If you could take care of him too, Madame Clarisse Georges, unless it's too late. Fabrice has to recite his verbs, he doesn't know them, he stutters. Yet he learned them well, with two or three other boarders who stayed in detention all weekend. But now he can't remember them. When M. Ziniac yelled very loudly right in front of him we all moved our desks back without meaning to. With M. Ziniac we all had the runs at eight a.m. on Mondays. I was, you were, he was, we were, I was a quiet, unassuming child, Madame Clarisse Georges, and then that ended too. Fabrizio gets a slap every Monday, because he doesn't have an unwed mother to punish him, it makes his nose bleed.

"Londerio, out!

M. Ziniac had a large signet ring and would hit kids with it when he was allowed to, he was coach of the upper school rugby team. I think M. Ziniac had blown a fuse, but no one could fix him. When he was in a good mood he told the kids he was having a house built for himself. Maybe it's the air that does it to them, I thought. When Uncle Jos returned from congresses he'd always say they were all crazy in Paris. Man digs his grave with his teeth! I wonder if Uncle Jos is right. In the evening, I look at myself, I check that I'm the same as before, my name is still Edgar and I'm growing up.

Then the period after it's my turn. I still can't draw. I don't do the geography maps. Mme. Allibert calls me to her desk as soon as we've put them back where they belong after M. Ziniac's class. She says Edgar, show me your map. I didn't do it. Then she takes her book and hits me over the head. She has social security glasses too, and wrinkles, and she's had it with us kids. When she wants to hit us over the head with the textbook, we have to bend down a little so she's able to do it, otherwise she gets even more angry. During exams, she knits with large needles. She gives a lot of exams. Once, Victor made a funny noise under his desk.

"Schpoc schpoc schpoc."

Mme. Allibert came over to him, pretending not to see anything.

"Schpoc schpoc schpoc."

Then she came back with her book and hit him on the head.

"Victor, put your tool back in!"

"Yes, Mme. Allibert."

"Schpoc schpoc schpoc."

Since it was a map we had to do, Edgar got a zero.

With Victor on Monday nights, after lights out and the verification of hands over sheets, we'd go out to the crematorium behind the prefab to make ourselves something to eat. Victor's mother had given him canned Olida pâté and Isabelle had given me some cheese, we took bread from the canteen to make toast. We set fires in the garbage cans. Victor's father had been a cook in another life, he didn't remember where. He moved a lot. And then we would return to the dormitory.

Fabrizio slept as soon as he lay down. At night, he prayed like a Dago kneeling in front of his bed and when Victor wasn't looking at me, I made Auntie Gina's sign of the cross on his forehead and he on mine, it could be useful for when we were grown up. But I don't want to tell you anymore, Madame Clarisse Georges. I don't like 1971, because of the decade that's already ended. The rest is too long, or too short, I wonder sometimes.

At night, with Fabrizio, we would tell each other stories. He had very white skin because he always stayed at boarding school even on holidays. He'd had several families before, but they'd all tossed out the baby with the bath water. It was his pigeon-toes, he'd say, or because he did so badly in school. He collected the little shiny white pebbles he found between the prefab and the gates of the boarding school. He liked when Edgar told him stories. He liked the ones about the Dutch people, the bones, the toads, and also my papa.

"My father is in Africa," I would say to him.

"Where?"

"In Mozambique. Which is between the name of a Shah

of Persia and the musician Mozart. In Mozambique, crocodiles run wild and eat people."

"And then what?" Fabrizio looked at his feet.

"My father, he's in Chad. He builds houses, the foundations are very deep, because of landslides and road workers
who are morons."

"And your mother?"

"Her name is Isabelle."

"And?"

"I don't know. She works in an office."

"Ah."

Fabrizio prefers crocodiles.

We go to the dining hall together. We pray for the meal,
scarf it down and then ask Lassale if we can watch TV. We're
tired of listening to his Breton guitar playing. If he doesn't let
us we have a fight, I stay behind Fabrice, we call each other
fucker and then after that we go sleep in the château. I was a
quiet, unassuming child but now my clothes are torn, you had
to fight all the time at boarding school. I ended up making
myself an unwed mother with my pillow too. I thought of
Uncle Jos, of Auntie Gina, I listened very hard, but didn't

remember. I couldn't hear them anymore. Yet when I tell my stories to Fabrizio, it's like I'm telling them to you, Madame Clarisse Georges, in case we see each other soon. But I heard the steps of the monitor, he was coughing, a drape separated us from his room. And then sometimes I guessed the words Maman didn't say, the crushed ones. JP talked enough for two, mind you, he thought boarding school was very good, I must've been well fed because I was a little too fat, and my ears, your son has big ears, Isa, I know, answered my maman Isabelle.

"He doesn't seem very bright. Mind you, when I was his age. . ."

Isabelle nodded, with the same gaze she's had since the dawn of time.

When we were alone in the evening, she and I, after the dishes Maman settled on the blue-gray armchair to read a novel, her favorite was still Madame Françoise Sagan and also the young Mademoiselle Albertine Sarrazin, an unwed mother without a kid whose love is Julien. I read them too, I had a lot of time on Sundays, and I liked them. On the cover Albertine had very short hair and black eyes, she was maybe a little bit Gypsy I thought, she'd broken a small bone in her ankle which sounds a little like the Astrakhan that's in Uncle Jos' party, and it had been the end for her. She wrote love letters to Julien. He was locked up like my papa. Maman was quiet. She slowly turned the pages, then she looked at her watch.

"Go to bed, Edgar." She turned her cheekbone toward me, almost without looking up from her book.

"What's the matter Edgar, go ahead, it's time!"

"Well yes."

Once, just before, I asked her again where my papa was. Maman closed her book and nodded her head, with her dark and traumatized eyes. Then she looked at me, and right at that moment, Madame Clarisse, I knew that I might not be president of Savoy when I grew up but that I'd do something stupid. She stood up and sighed, and then she went toward the new red sofa she'd bought with JP. Sometimes they sat there the two of them, there's no room for Edgar on it. They'd talk about their work. It's the glass ceiling, JP would say, the invisible hierarchy, yes, Isabelle nodded, exactly, it's the level of incompetence! Edgar's an idiot and kept bumping against it. In the closet next to it were large files where she kept all the forms and the bills with dates. When she wasn't there, I opened the closet without daring to look inside. She brought out a red file from the bottom of the stack like the ones where they use to file reports on the kids at boarding school, she told me to sit next to her. She pulled out a letter and also, stapled to it, a check she hadn't cashed. Then she read the letter. So I no longer had a papa, and you know Edgar, it hasn't been easy raising a noodle like you on my own. Edgar understood everything.

"Go on, go to bed now, go."

I took the bus to boarding school, Maman hardly spoke that year and what's more, JP'd had it, he wanted to go out and have fun, she took her pills in half a glass of water and nodded. I know, I know, Edgar didn't like this decade anymore at all. JP wore sunglasses when we rode in the car, he always turned on the radio, at one point we crossed the Seine and then, next to the statue of the old guy and the Tricycle cinema, which I hadn't been to yet, we took the Asnières Bridge toward Paris. My father is in the movies, I'd told Fabrizio.

But he'd looked at me right away with his look from Rue d'Avron and laughed in the direction of his pigeon-toed feet, that—that couldn't be true because I didn't have a photo. We arrived at the bus stop near Rue d'Amsterdam. Isabelle and JP turned their cheekbones toward me.

"Don't forget your things, Edgar."

"Well yes."

"See you soon."

JP went to wait in the car. That guy, I think, couldn't have been anyone's papa, he didn't like kids at all, with Edgar no matter how hard you tried you couldn't talk about anything, especially on Sundays which were for enjoying yourself, not for being miserable. I looked at Isabelle, her handbag against her arm, when I raised my hand, she shook her head. JP had lit a cigarette and was talking to her. He wanted to go out and get his mind off things, they really needed it after putting up with Edgar for a whole Sunday.

The bus took off, and if you want my opinion, the Seine, if you looked at it closely, had changed a lot, even if it was still as gray as ever, with troughs and swells under the wind, and on the banks, there were guys taking walks and Sunday lovers and people with their dogs. Isabelle looked at me just once this time, and I said to myself Edgar, president of Savoy, shit, Madame Clarisse, I don't remember anymore what I said to myself, on Edgar's word. In any case, I loved the bus. I opened my red bag, which I always placed next to me so I wouldn't completely forget it and I immediately unwrapped the chocolate bar that she'd given me for the week. Victor always wanted to melt it over the trash can but he'd pinch half of it. I also had a sandwich, two bananas, and a block of gruyere from the Monoprix supermarket next to the train station. The bus went very fast, the kids in the back got up and would kneel on the seats and make faces at people, but not Edgar. If you want to know what I think, Madame Clarisse, Paris is a place that's very very big in 1971, now I knew the bus route all the way to Argenteuil but after, there were factories, warehouses, and projects, then only houses and trees, it became more complicated. Aunt Meige, I thought to myself as I scarfed my chocolate, but no, I changed my mind.

We arrived at the gates and Father Duluc already had his black notebook in his hand.

"Hello Father!" we said.

The boarders went up the path and we started to talk about the things we'd done, I didn't have the dictionary from the common room with me. Fabrizio was picking up pebbles by the water, he came toward me feet first to show them to me. I don't know if he believed me right away, but I told him I was there to say goodbye, I'd only come back because of the bus and to give him my chocolate. He'd received candy the week before, he'd given me some.

"You're stupid, Edgar, you'll never make it."

Vavi ta more vavi ta more. I called Auntie Gina to get her opinion but she was doing her crossword and Uncle Jos was watching TV or maybe he was fixing the boiler under his cap. Anyway, they didn't answer. Fabrice didn't want to come with me but we still did the Dago sign of the cross on our foreheads to give ourselves courage. Then he went back to the others to hide the chocolate, I even gave him the picture that was inside, on Edgar's word. Father Duluc went back inside the house of the Fathers and the guard closed the gate. The little door next to it stayed open until ten for the monitors. I looked again but I didn't see my friend Victor, who wasn't in fact my friend as I explained to you, but we cooked pâté together, it creates a bond. Well then, I said to myself, shit, I can't remember what I said to myself.

In any case I took off fast, like for the retreat at Stalingrad, and right away, not being all there, I had a hard time finding the way to Enghien, where the casino gamblers go and drown in the lake on the weekends and on Monday go back to work. Victor used to stroll there with his mother, he was good at skipping stones. I remembered the way to the train, though. I had a little money that I'd taken from JP because I was a thief in the making like my father, and I bought a ticket to Paris.

*

I took a quick look around the train car. There were a lot of open seats, so I chose one by an old lady with a black bag on her lap and a black coat like the ones old Dago women at Uncle Jos and Auntie Gina's wore. I put my satchel with the shoulder straps on top of my bag and then I put my feet on top, because I needed to keep track of it. When we get near Paris the houses change, they become buildings and the city is lit up. I thought to myself that I would see the Seine, it was very beautiful this time, on Edgar's word. Then the train slows down and there're lots of different tracks crossing each other and it makes your ears happy, mine squealed all over. I thought of Aunt Meige, who was a shorthand typist on trains, but it wasn't the right station. I also had métro tickets. First I had to put my satchel with the shoulder straps back on and with my big red bag I had a hard time going through the turnstiles. I also thought a little about Isabelle, maybe she was reading a book, or else she'd gone to JP's in his car. We would see each other again soon, once I was grown up, we'd look at each other in the evening when it was time to go to bed and it would be as good as the Parc Monceau, or I'd take her to the go-see road and she'd go pick wild flowers. When I'm the president she won't take her pink pills that make her swallow words and look at me like that anymore. We could talk for a long time about before. For the moment I wanted to leave her alone, but I made a mistake in the métro, and I ended up at Gare de Lyon. There, I had a real hard time. It wasn't like with Aunt Meige or before when I was little. When I looked at the tracks, people were walking in every direction,

I even saw policemen. On the departures board the letters of the destinations were changing very fast and making a funny noise. And then, suddenly, there was a new place on the board, with a new time for going there. After that I saw soldiers and I thought that maybe Uncle Jos was having a congress, that we'd run into each other, but no. Then, I had the urge to piss, but I couldn't find the men's room because the station was so large. There was a big café like the kind Aunt Meige used to take me to sometimes on the Boulevards but I had no one to help me get down the stairs. I wanted to cry and call Maman, but you know, on Edgar's word, I held back. Instead I left with my satchel because I was afraid of missing the train, even though it wasn't leaving until the next day. I pissed outside the station, I had just enough time to finish before picking up my bag, because the street was kind of steep behind the line of taxis, I don't know if you know that. I again saw some policemen, who usually had mustaches that year, and then I exited the Gare de Lyon, to go see the Seine before taking my train. I'm eleven now, for a long time we've been meant to see each other, I want to show you how much I've grown up.

I didn't dare ask how to get to the Seine, though, so I walked straight ahead. Maybe I'd land at Aunt Meige's and she'd take me straight there the next day. At one point I was afraid I wouldn't find the Gare de Lyon again, but when I turned I saw the tall clock tower at Tour de L'Horloge that's there so you won't miss your train, so I was able to keep going. And there, Madame Clarisse, I finally saw the monument with the Génie statue that looks like it's all made of gold, where the Parisians knocked down the prison from which it seems to fly away, and the Seine is right next to it, Edgar president! The river had lots of colors at night with lighter spots and there are no dams in Paris. Nobody drowns. And life preservers are hooked to the banks, with a rope coiled in the middle. I'll put some on the fences at the Findus warehouses when I'm president. I went down with my satchel, and I was really very happy to be there. It runs far away.

My name is Edgar, I was born at Rue d'Avron. I watched boats go all the way to the end while waiting to take the train. I put down my satchel, there was no one around, so I opened my red bag and ate my ham sandwich. On the other side, there was no one either, except the people walking dogs that were sniffing between the trees. And after that I felt like eating some more chocolate, but I'd given the rest to Fabrizio. I was a little afraid, even though I'm grown up. I'm going to return to Uncle Jos and Auntie Gina's and we'll walk a long time along the go-see road with Isabelle, JP won't come because she'll have dumped him. In his letter my papa had beautiful handwriting in big block letters, as if he'd been an idiot too at Rue d'Avron before me. He must have made a big effort to write in block letters, but in fact I don't know. One day, can I know? I tried to sing *avanti popolo bandiera rossaaa!* but I was afraid someone would hear me who was against Uncle Jos's party, and that would've been the end of it all. I was a little sleepy, Madame Clarisse George, but I didn't cry, on Edgar's word. It was just mostly that after a while I was afraid I wouldn't be able to find Gare de Lyon again. I picked up my things and I continued along the Seine, walking faster and faster, but then I looked up at the Génie and from where I was I could still see the clock tower, so I went a different way. I was used to roads that always go in the same direction, like the go-see or the bus route or even Rue d'Asnières that follows the train tracks and on the left there's the Monoprix. There was no one around, and I went back up. I finally saw a man who wasn't walking his dog, maybe the dog had run away too.

"Hello sir," I said, "I'm at boarding school. I'm looking for Gare de Lyon."

The man was wearing half-frame glasses and was carrying a book in the pocket of his raincoat and a newspaper in his hand.

"Where are you going?"

"I'm going to take my train at Gare de Lyon."

"Gare de Lyon?"

"Well yes," I answered, because you know Edgar.

I had the scare of the century for that year when he told me that he was going to Gare de Lyon too. His name was M. Berthier. So I said good evening Monsieur Berthier, he had a lot of wrinkles on his forehead when he bent down to say to me, what's wrong? I thought he meant my drooping ears or my nose that was growing too fast for my face, but no, it was just that he found my eyes strange.

"Are you crying?"

"Well, it's because of Gare de Lyon."

"What's your name?" Monsieur Berthier asked me.

And then, Madame Clarisse Georges, I answered Edgaaar, moo. . . Edgaaarrr. . .

"Calm down. Edgar, is that it?"

"Well yes."

Then he took my bag and we went to Gare de Lyon.

"Where is your boarding school? Where are your parents?"

"Well yes," I answered.

M. Berthier was a strange guy, if you want my opinion. But since he's so old you probably didn't know him at Rue d'Avron. He sat down in the big bar and summoned a waiter he called *garçon* with a snap of his fingers and he took off his gloves, like he was afraid of germs from the end of the world. I remembered that Uncle Jos also wore gloves when he went to Paris. He put down my red bag.

"We shall have something to drink, Edgar. Then we shall see."

I bawled silently, with my not being all there swirling like confetti, and I still had the scare of the century. So I said all kinds of nonsense to him.

"Are you hungry? Would you like an ice cream? A pastry?"

M. Berthier ate his ice cream and I drank a glass of grenadine because he was crazy enough to eat ice cream in December but not Edgar, your humble servant.

"You must have a papa, a maman?"

"Well no," I said.

"And your boarding school?"

"Well, I'm going there," I told M. Berthier.

But he answered me, no, we were staying here. He finished his ice cream, I still didn't want one, then he took me to pee downstairs. After that we went along the platforms, there weren't too many more departing trains. He was carrying my red bag and I ended up telling M. Berthier who kept asking me the same question that I lived on Rue d'Avron.

"Rue d'Avron? What number? Do you have a phone number then?"

"Well no, Edgar the noodle answered, I've lived at Rue d'Avron since my birth."

"Since your birth?"

"Well yes."

I was all flushed now, like Isabelle when she played cards long ago in Ménilmontant. At the end of the platforms, we entered a place with a tinted glass door, and Edgar had the scare of the century because it was full of policemen. M. Berthier held me by the neck, but without squeezing too hard.

Gentlemen, good evening; he removed his gloves this time.

A guy with a mustache and a big belly got up and looked at me, the Edgar package, who'd missed his train to go back home.

"This young man seems to me to be greatly perturbed. He says his name is Edgar."

"Yes, said the guy with the mustache. And you, are you family?"

"Not only am I not his family, but I have no family. I only came to accompany him."

"Ah. All right. What's your name, Edgar?" The guy with the mustache asked me.

"Edgaaarr," I bellowed.

"Edgar is that it?"

"Well yes."

And then he came toward me.

"I'm not going to hurt you, buddy. Take off your parka, you're too hot."

I was labeled all over because of boarding school. After that M. Berthier offered his card and asked that he be kept informed and the guy with the mustache said yes, he wasn't alone in the office. They took me to the back room, I sat down at a table.

"All right. Let's play. What do you want to play?"

I gave him my super moron look.

The guy with the mustache who'd talked to M. Berthier gave me some sheets of paper with République Française marked at the top, whereas for me it was just Savoy. He told me, draw, if you like. Then he spoke to someone on the phone, saying my name, calling one precinct and another, and then another again, he's about ten or eleven, he described how I was dressed and my distinguishing marks, and there, I was really surprised, he didn't even notice.

"I'll hold, yes, yes. I'm not hanging up. I know I know." He really had the big belly of a guy with a mustache and was smoking a Gauloise. When he turned around toward me, he winked.

"You sure you don't want to draw?"

I had brown hair, I was the height of a child my age, I was born in Paris, Rue d'Avron, at Hôpital de la Croix Saint-Simon. Oh no, no, he said. He has his school bag, his things too, a red bag. A boarding school student? That's right, yes, that's right. I listened hard with my ears wide open to find out who he was talking to. You're sending someone? What?

I'm in the waiting room at Rue d'Avron. I hope it really is you I'm going to see, Madame Clarisse Georges.

"No, he's just a kid, said the guy with the mustache. What? Bah, a little, I don't know. . . He crushed his cigarette and showed me the trash can, because Edgar who was not all there had torn up the paper. No, he's quiet, yes yes, no problem, we'll wait, we'll wait. Nice.

Afterward, I opened my red bag and ate the cheese Isabelle had given me for the week at boarding school. I won't have lost anything at all this time.

"Is this the first time you've gone off on your own like this?"

"Well yes."

"You have a funny accent."

"Well yes, I answered, I'm Edgar, president of Savoy."

"Well well, said the guy with the mustache. Your parents are on their way, they'll be here soon."

The guy with the mustache stopped. Someone had opened the door.

"Hold on, there's someone here, I have to go see what it is. I'll leave you here, be good."

"Well yes."

The guy with the mustache stood up.

"I'll be back. Stay right here."